FORCE OF KNIGHT MAGIC

FORCE OF NATURE SERIES BOOK 3

KATHI S. BARTON

SECOND EDITION

WCP

World Castle Publishing, LLC
Pensacola, Florida

Copyright © Kathi S. Barton 2012
ISBN: 9781938961328
First Edition World Castle Publishing, LLC October 1, 2012
Second Edition World Castle Publishing, LLC October 20, 2013
http://www.worldcastlepublishing.com

Cover: Karen Fuller
Photos: Shutterstock
Editor: Brieanna Robertson

CHAPTER 1

Phil stood outside the hotel room for several minutes before he could work up the nerve to knock. She was going to be upset; more than that, she was going to be pissed at her brother too. He moved to the door, and had raised his hand to knock when it was jerked open…and there she stood.

Phil Campbell would never be able to see her without his breath catching. She was beautiful, yes, but it was more than that. Her body, her scent, called to him. He needed her, needed her with every bone, every cell…hell, every part of his body. She was his mate, his other half, and they both knew it. And her standing there fresh from what he assumed was a shower, with her bath robe on, made him think that her brother had the right idea in telling Phil to just claim her.

Holly Force was a werewolf. Her sister-in-law CJ, who was now married to the pack's alpha and Holly's brother, Austin, had been his good friend long before he'd met the entire family. Phil had known about Holly, but had never thought to approach her as his mate because she was a wolf and he a vampire. But a long talk with her brother had made him realize that if he didn't claim her he'd never be happy.

"What the hell are you doing here?" Before he could answer her, there was a small ding behind him, signaling the elevator coming to a stop on this floor. Turning to see who got off, he nearly lost his balance when he was suddenly jerked inside the room and the door was closed behind them.

She had him pressed against the wall and her hand over his mouth before he could begin to understand that she was hiding him. Her breath on his neck when she leaned in and whispered in his ear to be quiet nearly made him whimper, and he did reach out and wrap his hand around her waist, bringing her flush against him.

"Don't," was all she said before he heard someone coming down the hallway. When the person stopped at the door, Phil ran his tongue down Holly's throat to the pulse that was beating fast, and took in as much of her scent as he could.

"Tell them to go away," Phil told her in a whisper when the person knocked. "Tell them you're busy and that you'll talk to them later." He nipped at her earlobe, cupped her ass in his hand, and rocked into her before he scraped his teeth along the vein.

"I can't. Christ, don't do that." In a louder voice, she spoke to who he thought was on the other side of the door. "I'm running just a little behind, darling, just give me—" Her moan broke free and he had to smile.

Phil didn't care what she thought she was going to do; she wasn't leaving this room until they at least talked. But with her body pressed against his and his cock hard as stone, he figured it would be hours before they even spoke if he had anything to do with it. He turned her so that she was backed against the wall and he cupped her breast in his hand.

"I want to taste you, Holly. I want to make love to you right here and anywhere else that—"

"I can't, damn it." She pulled away and he let her; he would never force anyone. "Don't move. I have to try and salvage this or I'll be…damn it, how the hell did you find me anyway?"

Her voice was low, low enough that unless the person on the other side was a supernatural, he'd not hear a word. Phil was just about to tell her that he was there because he needed her when the person on the other side spoke for the first time.

"Come on, Heather. I know you're still a mite pissed at me about last night, but you said that you'd give me another go. I'll not touch you like that again. You have my word on it as a gentleman." Phil looked from her to the door. With a raised brow he started to the door, but was pressed back against the wall with a knife to his throat.

"Don't move or so help me, I'll end you." He didn't move. Not because he was afraid she'd do it, but because he didn't want to hurt her. She was strong, yes…all weres were…but he was stronger and much bigger than her. She might hurt him, but in the end, he knew that he could take her if need be. And he was counting on the fact that, as his mate, she really couldn't do much more than push him around.

Moving the blade from his throat without taking his eyes from hers, he glanced at the door then back at her again. "Finish this with him then we talk. I'm your mate and you won't be going anywhere with him."

"I will go where I want, when I want, and if you think that will ever change because you think you're my mate then you're stupider than the guy at the door." She moved away and toward the door without another word. The door opened, and the chain still in place kept him from seeing the stupid person on the other side. But his voice, his scent, wasn't anything Phil would ever forget.

"There you are," the man said, relief in his voice. "I thought we had a date tonight. I got reservations at the hotel dining room. Come on out and let's eat a hardy dinner. I have plans tonight."

Phil walked up beside Holly, not revealing himself to the man at the door. He could touch her all he wanted and he did so. Cupping her breast that was hidden from view, Phil leaned down and nuzzled it with his mouth. Her fingers lacing in his hair was all the warning he got before she yanked his head up hard.

"Oh, baby, you have to let me get a few things figured out. You're a mite early." She looked over at Phil and he could see the hatred in her eyes. Whether for him or the man on the other side, he wasn't sure, but it didn't stop him from taking advantage of her distraction.

The kiss was brief and left him wanting more. He was about to take another nibble of her lower lip when she brought her heel down on his foot. Staggering back, he decided that if she wanted to play, then he would play too.

Taking her wrist into his hand, he pulled it to his mouth. He licked the rapid beating pulse before he scraped his fangs over the sensitive area and drew blood. He knew that this was wrong, but he wanted her in the worst way and tasting her would give him an advantage. But before he could taste the warmth that trickled from her tiny wound, she jerked free and punched him in the nose.

"Heather? Are you all right? What's going on?" Phil had his hand over his nose and mouth, trying to stop the flow of blood, when he realized that the man was calling her Heather and not Holly. He pulled her as close as he could and put his mouth to her ear.

"Who is this and what the hell does he want with you? He isn't here to see you as a were or he'd know who you were. What the fuck is going on?" She lifted his chin up as he finished speaking. She looked pissed, but this time he could tell that it was with the man on the other side of the door.

"I can't come out tonight. I have to pack up. I told you that this morning. But if you want to get a drink at the bar…just give me ten minutes, sugar, and I'll be right down." The man on the other side cursed. "It's the best I can do. You had an opportunity last evening, but you went and screwed that up all on you—"

"Come on, Heather. I need to see you. I've got something to tell you, something that I just gotta tell somebody or I'm gonna bust." The man leaned against the door and had Phil ready to attack, but Holly stopped him with a squeeze of her hand on his shoulder and a small shake of her head. "Please, honey. Just one more chance?"

"All right. Dinner and nothing more. I do have to catch a plane in the morning and I have to get my beauty rest." She smiled at the man at the door before starting to close it. "I'll meet you in the bar in ten minutes."

"You don't need any more beauty sleep, darling, but I'll behave. I promise. I'll be waiting for you. You might wanna change your mind about leaving me after you hear what I have to tell you." His voice seemed to move away from the door and Phil knew it when he heard the ding again. "See you in ten then."

Phil waited until he heard the elevator move down the shaft before he thought about what he wanted to say to her. He had wanted to do this calmly, but that wasn't even an option right now. Looking over at Holly when she started pulling things out of a suitcase, Phil grabbed her and threw her on the bed.

~~~

She didn't need this right now. Not tonight anyway. She looked up at the handsome man laying over her and wanted so badly to claim him, to have him bite her. She fisted her hand at her side before she gave in to the fact that she wanted to touch him, run her fingers through his hair, and kiss him.

"I have to get ready. I have nine minutes to meet him downstairs for—" His mouth covered hers and she opened up before she could think that she shouldn't.

Christ, the man could kiss. His mouth fit over hers like it was made to be there...which she supposed, in the grand scheme of things, it was. When his hand slid up her thigh, she moaned and gripped the blanket beneath her.

"I want you. Now. I want to sink my cock deep inside of you and not stop until neither of us can move." He rocked into her soft flesh and she moaned again. "Holly, please say yes. Please tell me that you want me as much as I want you."

She did, that was the problem. But getting to the hotel bar was more important. At least to her job it was. She took advantage of his moving mouth and tried to reason with him. But the moment he moved the robe from her breast and suckled on her nipple, she couldn't have told him her name if he'd asked.

"Phil, please? I have to talk to you. I have to—holy Christ." He bit her. Not enough to be really painful, but enough for her to want more. She grabbed his hair again and pulled him up. "Stop that right now. I have to go. You've no idea what you've stepped into, and I don't have time to explain right now."

He lifted his body up, but all that did was press his hard cock harder into her pussy. She tried to be pissed, but she knew he could smell her, smell that she was aroused. He grinned down at her and she knew a moment of pure love, but pushed it away. She couldn't love him, not now.

"I have to go to the bar and meet that man. I don't have a choice." She tried to shove him off her, but all he did was lean down and kiss her again. She nearly gave in again. It was getting harder by the second. "You don't understand. I don't—"

"You have a choice. Everyone does. Yours is to either stay here with me and let me make love to you all night long, or I go down to the bar and drain the bastard." He grinned again. "That second choice has a great deal of appeal to me right now."

She shoved him harder and he rolled off her. She was sure it was because he allowed her to, not because she was stronger than him. He watched her rise and she flushed when she saw how much of her body he'd exposed. She glared at him as she grabbed up her pants again.

"You're a pain in the ass." She moved toward the bathroom as she continued. "I have to go. If you don't...Phil, what are you doing here?" That thought had just occurred to her. How had he found her, and who the hell else knew where she was? When he got up and sauntered toward her, she knew that she wasn't going to like his answer. When he kissed her lightly on the mouth and walked toward the suitcase that now lay on the floor, she watched him, waiting.

"Who is this guy and why is he calling you Heather? I'm guessing that he doesn't know you're a were either, does he?" She shook her head at his question, knowing she couldn't lie to him. "And last night, he tried something that pissed you off enough that you'd leave the chain on the door to speak to him because why...you don't trust that he won't try it again?"

She nodded this time before answering. "He backed me against the wall and tried to take more than I was willing to give. Well, that's not true. He tried to take everything. And before you ask, no, I didn't do anything wolf-like on his ass. I simply pushed him away."

"No, you didn't," he said laughingly. "You did do something. No man comes begging at a woman's door for forgiveness if she only pushed him away." He walked to her, slipped his hand under the robe, and cupped her breast. "What did you do to him, love? Tell me the truth and I won't go down there and take his throat out with my bare hands."

She swallowed hard. He'd made it sound like he was going to the corner for a loaf of bread. And she knew that if she didn't answer him or didn't tell him what she'd actually done to him, he'd do just what he said.

"I punched him in the mouth, then I kicked his balls up around his eyes." She licked her lips when he moved his mouth closer to hers. "I...are you going to kiss me, Phil?"

"Do you want me to?" She nodded. "Then no. If we both are willing then you aren't leaving this room. And the sooner you get this guy taken care of, the sooner you can explain to me why he's so important and why he doesn't know your name."

Holly took a step back, then another. She moved to the bathroom and only stopped when he said her name. Just managing to catch the pants she'd had in her hand before another piece of material came toward her, she looked up at him when he cleared his throat.

"You now have less than five minutes. I would hurry if I were you, and if you come out of there with something that I don't think is covering enough of you, you won't leave even then."

She closed the door but didn't lock it. She wasn't sure if she wanted him to come in and take her or if she thought it didn't matter. He'd come in if he wanted, and no lock would stop him. She leaned against the counter and looked at herself. Christ, she looked like she'd been rolling in a bed with a man, and had that almost satisfied look on her face. She pulled the shirt, a heavy sweater she could see now, over her head with a smile. Phil talking from the other side of the door made her faster in fixing her hair.

"Who is he?" he asked her. "And why should I not follow you down to the bar and make sure that he behaves himself?"

Biting her lip, she pulled on her pants. She was zipping them up when she answered, hoping what she said would be enough to satisfy him. She didn't think she could hold him off for long, but it was worth a shot.

"He's a client. Someone that I have to…he has something I need, and this is the only way I can get it. It should take me a few hours so if you wanted to leave, I can talk to you tomorrow." She held her breath, hoping he'd say okay. "Then we can have a talk then."

"What sort of client? He doesn't strike me as the buyer type. I'm not sure what you're selling, but whatever it is, he's more of the taking sort of guy." Holly closed her eyes on how true his words were. "What's his name?"

"Jasper Clayton. And he is a buyer. I just need to get some information from him for someone else. But he's proving to be stubborn about it." She opened the door and nearly fell into Phil's arms. "You should just go on back home. I'll be home in a few days."

"No. What is he buying from you?" He was using compulsion and she could feel the need to answer him…overwhelmingly so. She tried to move away from him, but he pulled her tighter. "Answer me, Holly."

She leaned her head on his chest, suddenly very tired. She'd been working like this, at this same job, since she'd gotten out of high school and had taken those stupid tests to apply for a job with The Office. Little had she known that she'd be working at doing something like this all these years later.

"I can't tell you." When he stiffened, she hurried on. "I can't. Not now. I…damn it, Phil, do you have any idea how much trouble I can get into if someone knew I told you? They could have me…." She looked up at him. "Who told you I was here?"

"Gordon. He said he knows where you are every time you leave. He doesn't know what you're doing, but he always knows where you are." He moved back when she did. "What are you not telling me? I can protect you, Holly. I need to. You're my mate. I can't let anything happen to you."

Coming to a decision, she nodded at him. "All right. When I get back. If you're still here, I'll tell you…I'll tell you everything. Then afterwards, if you want to leave, I'll understand." She tried to straighten her shoulders to show him that it mattered little to her if he stayed or not, but she could see that he knew she was bluffing.

"And do I get something to help me know if I stay or go? Something that I can…I don't know, give me a hint as to why I'd want to leave the only woman I'm ever going to love?"

"I work as an undercover agent for the Central Intelligence Agency as a hired assassin." She smiled at the look on his face. "And the man downstairs is someone I have to get information from before I have to put a bullet between his eyes."

Holly walked out the door and to the elevator. She stepped in just as Phil came out of her room and leaned against the doorjamb. She held open the door knowing that he was going to tell her goodbye. She should have known better.

"I'll be here when you get back. And for the record…."

She waited for him to continue before letting go of the door.

"When you kill him, I'm going to be there with you."

CHAPTER 2

The target moved into the bar about ten minutes later than he thought she might. There wasn't any time frame tonight that he knew of, only that she had to be dead by this time tomorrow. He watched her walk across the floor and wondered how anything so sexy could be so deadly. She moved to his contact, and he sat back to watch him try and handle her.

She'd bested him last night. Frank had seen her take him down and still laughed about it. He sat up in his chair, hoping to see another show tonight. She was way out of Clayton's league. Hell, if he really wanted to be honest, she might even be out of his. He looked down at the folder that was open in front of him.

Holly Force: age unknown. Address: unknown. Place of birth: unknown. He smiled at the one bit of information that they did have. Place of employment: agent. They weren't even sure which agency she worked for. But they knew for a fact that it wasn't for them. They'd have kept her under lock and key if she had been.

Frank McGuire wanted to bring her in alive and see what they could find out about the beautiful woman, but his boss said no. They were better off with her dead and forgotten rather than bringing her in and trying to convert her. Frank didn't want to convert her; he wanted to fuck her.

When Holly followed Clayton to the table, he adjusted the microphone in his ear. He could now hear everything that was being said at the little table in the corner, and the men on the other side of their table—on the other side of the wall, really—were recording everything he might miss. Frank had all the bases covered. He listened to what Clayton said and hoped they'd get the answers they needed. If not, he would let her kill this man—he was growing more useless all the time—and then he'd follow her back to her room, fuck her brains out, then kill her as well. All good in his book.

"Heather, you've no idea how sorry I am about last night. I don't know what came over me. You're so lovely and I'd had too much to drink that I just…well, I just forgot myself." Frank wanted to gag at Clayton's tone of voice, too sweet and syrupy for his taste. "You have the loveliest eyes."

Looking down at the photo of her that lay on top of her dossier, he agreed with Clayton's assessment of her eyes. They were the most brilliant shade of gold he'd ever seen.

"Look, big boy, we're here to have dinner together, and you had something to tell me. Tell me so that I can decide if I stay another day or I move on back to where I came from."

Frank snickered at her tone. She was one ballsy bitch.

He looked down again at the folder. He wasn't sure why the men upstairs thought she was a hired gun. To him she looked like every wet dream every male from the age of fifteen on up had had about a beautiful woman. Big eyes, bigger boobs, and an ass that you could bounce a quarter off and have it land in your beer a table away.

"And where is that? Hum? You've never told me anything about you. Where you're from? What you do?"

Frank waited, holding his breath.

"We've known each other for all of five hours, so when is it exactly that I was supposed to share with you?" She snorted. "Never mind, it doesn't matter. What is it you wanted to tell me?"

"Tell you? Oh yeah, the big news." He leaned toward her and Frank had the sudden urge to go over and pound Clayton's head against the table. Several times. Hard. "I'm going to come into some big money soon."

They were working on the angle that she might follow Clayton back to his room, on the assumption that she was a money hungry bitch. Personally, Frank didn't think it would fly, but he was only there as support and not calling the shots. He glanced up when a tall man moved to the bar, then promptly dismissed him. He had bigger fish to kill.

"Big money? How big, and—" Even from across the room, he could see her stiffen. He wondered about it for all of a few seconds until she started talking again. "Where did you get all your big money?"

"I've been working. On this deal, see, and it's about to pay off." Clayton reached over and touched her shoulder, and Frank heard a low growl like a wild beast was in the room. He looked around when Clayton did, wondering if he'd heard it too. "Did you hear that? It sounded like a tiger or something."

"Or something. What did you do for a living that would only just now begin to pay off?" She looked nervous now and kept glancing around the room. Frank was suddenly very nervous himself and started to call his men in.

It happened fast. He'd swear that no one moved when the police questioned him later that night, but the blood said otherwise. When he felt the first warm splash hit him in the face, he didn't even wipe it away. He felt like a man in a dream, a horrific colorful dream where nothing would ever be right again.

Clayton was dead. That much did register to him immediately afterwards. He hadn't seen his actual death, but he had seen the aftermath. Clapping his hand over his mouth, he looked away. Yes, he hadn't liked the guy, but this....

"Christ," he muttered.

"You gonna be all right? You're sort of looking a little green there." Frank looked over at the cop sitting across from him to avoid looking at what was left of the men he'd come there with, who were strewn all over the room. "You said you didn't see anything. I was asking you how that was possible. There's a lot of mess here for no one to have seen it."

Frank had to agree, but that's exactly what had happened. Four of his men were dead, murdered in the most heinous way possible, and yet, here he sat. And another thing that bothered him was the woman. Where the hell had she gone?

Looking down to try and think what to tell the officer that was demanding answers, Frank knew that he had none to give him. That was when he noticed that the file was missing too. He knew it had been there when everything went bad, because a perfect outline of it was there on the table with blood all around where it had not been. He tried to think if he or the officer had moved it, and knew without much of a doubt that whoever had killed the men had also taken the woman and the file.

Frank was suddenly glad he was retiring after this one. He'd not thought about it before, but now seemed like a really good time; hell, a great time to get out. He had money saved and his eye on a piece of property he was going to buy in the islands just as soon as this ass let him go.

~~~

Phil opened the door to his room and shoved her inside. He was covered in blood and so was she. He sniffed the air and could find nothing more than the woman who'd come in to clean while he'd been gone today. He held Holly still, afraid that one of them would fall apart. And he was terrified that it was going to be him.

"I can't breathe." He loosened his grip on her but didn't let her go. "Phil, are you all right?"

"Yes. No." He took a deep breath. "I fucking have no idea. Just let me hold you a bit longer. I don't…I'm still trying to figure out what happened down there."

She pulled away and looked up at him. "That wasn't you?" He looked down at her and frowned. "You didn't kill those people?"

"No. I don't know…it was something else. Someone else. I don't…. Christ, all I could think about was getting you safe. Did you get any sense of who it was?"

"I don't know. I was having a conversation with my target when all of the sudden he—" She shivered in his arms. "All of the sudden, he was just gone."

Gone. A good word for what had happened. The man had been torn apart. His head had landed near his chair and his arm on the table next to him before Phil had moved to get Holly out of harm's way. He had only seen the file that he still had in his hand at the other man's table by chance. He tucked it into the back of his pants, not sure what it said, but knew that they had enough to deal with right now.

"The other people, did you know they were there too?" She shook her head then nodded. "Which is it, love? Did you know or not?" He smiled and knew that it was as strained-looking as it felt. Humor, he thought, wasn't really coming off right now. He pulled her head back to his chest. She snuggled into his neck and he tightened his grip on her. Christ, he wanted her.

"I could smell them. Not see…they were all over my target, their smell, I mean. Then I could smell someone else.

15

Not you, I could see you, but this person wasn't there. I think that the people that I couldn't see were already dead when we—I need a shower. Do you think it would be all right if I took one?"

She pulled away and he let her. When she went to the bath and closed the door behind her, he moved to the chair and sat down hard. When the door clicked behind him a few minutes later, he turned to look at her, steam billowing out behind her.

"Will you come and shower with me, Phil?" He didn't move as she continued. "Please? I need you to come and shower with me right now."

"If I do, Holly, I won't...I think you might be better off taking one alone. I will be here when you come out. I promise you, baby, I'm not going anywhere." His breath caught when she stepped out of the doorway naked. "Holly, please, honey. You're killing me, love. I want you too badly to—"

"Come to me, Phil. I know what I'm asking you. I want you to make love to me. I want you to take me. Please? I need to...I want you to make me feel alive again." She took a few steps toward him and he stood up. "Please? Please come and make love to me."

He walked toward her like a man in a trance. When he took her outstretched hand into his, he kissed it. He began unbuttoning his shirt one handed as he walked her backwards toward the door.

The bathroom was large. When he'd checked in earlier that morning, his first thought after seeing it was how much fun he and Holly could have in the biggest shower he'd ever seen. He cupped the back of her neck now and brought her mouth to his.

She tasted of sweet wine. The glass she'd had in front of her had been a ruby red in the bar, and he now knew that it had been a chateau…a warm, dark red. But it was the flavor beneath that he was savoring.

Her tongue slid along his and he lifted her up and sat her on the counter. Her small hands moved down the buttons on his silk shirt until he felt her hands skim along his chest. When she touched his nipple, he pulled his mouth away to watch what she was doing to him.

"Your skin is warm. I didn't…I'm sorry, I thought you'd be cold." He grinned at her when she flushed. "You must think I'm so stupid."

"No. No, I don't. I think you're beautiful." He moaned when she licked at his areola and hissed through his teeth when she bit him. "My skin is getting a lot hotter too."

He desperately wanted her to touch him everywhere, but he needed to slow her down. If she kept this up, he'd be inside of her sooner than he wanted. Well, sooner than she would be ready for him.

"Lay back on the counter for me. I want to taste you." She looked up at him with glazed eyes and his fangs burst through his gums. "Holly, I'm going to eat your pussy, lay back for me."

He opened her legs as he got down on his knees before her. He could smell her scent and it called to him. Licking her thigh to just where her leg met her hip, he slid his hand up to her trimmed soft nether lips.

"Have you ever had a man eat you before?" She shook her head at his question. "Good. I'm going to drink from you, lick you, and drink your nectar when you come. Then when you're ready, I'm going to slide my cock deep into you and take you. Do you know what that means?"

"You're going to bite me and then drink my blood. Will I be your mate then?" Her voice made his cock jump in his jeans. "Will I be able to bite you too, Phil?"

"Yes," he told her. "When you come with me, I'm going to give you my wrist and you'll drink from me while I take from your throat. Holly, if this isn't what you want, now is the time to tell me."

He waited for her to speak, waited for her answer. He'd never want her to feel that she had no choice. And he'd never forgive himself if she thought she didn't. He didn't touch her again as he watched her; emotions ran across her face quickly.

"I don't know. I want you, but I don't know if...I don't want you to think I'm only teasing you." He nearly whimpered at her when she leaned back again. "I want you to make love to me, but I'm...I don't think I'm ready for anything more right now. Understand?"

In answer, he slid his finger deep inside of her and watched her face. When her eyes fluttered closed, he let them. As much as he wanted to see her eyes change when she came, he didn't want her to see how much she was hurting him. Lowering his head to where his fingers were dancing inside of her, Phil took his first taste of paradise.

She came within seconds; his small bit of compulsion when he told her to come was all it took. He took his fill of her cum as it poured from her body. Over and over he drank from her until she sobbed for him to stop. He thought she'd come at least half a dozen times and he still wanted to give her more. Standing now, he tore his pants open and freed his cock.

"Please. I want to feel you deep inside of me. Please, Phil. I want to feel you deep." He wanted to give her what she wanted, but knew that if he took her now he'd bite, and as much as he wanted to come deep inside of her heat, he didn't want to taste her without permission. "Please."

"I can't, baby. I want to come on you. I want to—mother fuck." She pushed him to the floor. Before he could try to ascertain what had happened, she had straddled him and his cock was at her entrance. "Holly, don't. If you do that, you're mine. I'll be your mate and—"

She screamed out his name as she impaled herself over him. He was buried as deep as he could be inside of her. He held her hips still as she sat there. His cock felt strangled as her body adjusted to his size. She lifted her head finally and looked down at him, tears streaming down her face.

"You weren't going to make love to me, were you?" He shook his head. "I told you that I wanted you, just not for us to exchange blood. Why?"

He flipped her over to her back and he rocked deep inside of her. "Because we're mated now. Even if I don't take your blood, which I want to more than my next breath, I can still claim you by filling you with my seed." He rocked again, harder this time, and she moaned with him. "I'm going to fill you, Holly. And then I'm going to take your throat. You took me; I'm going to take you."

He moved slowly at first, feeling her sheath hug him. Then as she moved with each of his strokes, he moved faster, harder, deeper into her. Taking her breast into his mouth, he scraped his fangs over the hard tip and then suckled it. Running his hand up her throat, he moved her so that he could bite, knowing that he couldn't take her this way. Never would he take what she did not freely offer.

"Come, Holly. Come now." Even as she climaxed once, twice, and then a third time, he felt his fangs stretch, the need to claim hard on him as he came with her. When she slipped away, fell into an exhausted sleep, he took her wrist to his mouth. "So that I can watch over you."

The bite was small. She didn't even flinch when he pierced her skin. The blood, however small an amount, was enough. He would be able to find her anywhere and at any time. He knew it was wrong, but after today he simply didn't care.

Lifting her up, Phil took her to the still running shower. She woke a little, but not fully, so he did most of the work himself. By the time he'd washed her hair with his shampoo and then rinsed it, he was hard again. He doubted that he'd ever get enough of her. Laying her onto his bed, Phil dressed again. He had to go and find out what he could about the carnage downstairs.

CHAPTER 3

There were enough cops and other official personnel around that it would be small wonder if they were able to collect anything but cop DNA. Myles looked around the room again and thought that maybe this was the worst crime scene he'd ever been on. Yeah, he thought, it was worse than that bus accident a few years ago where fifty-three people had been killed.

"Sarge, there's a guy here to see you. Says he might have something about the case you'd be interested in." Myles looked at the officer before looking to where he pointed. "He said his name is Gregory Hooper."

Myles took the information that the cop had written down and read it. Gregory Hooper was a retired detective from Georgia. The man was standing by the yellow tape that stopped most of the people from coming in, and Myles could see that he was probably a lot older than he looked. He wasn't sure why he thought that, but figured he'd listen to what he had to say. He walked over to him and took his hand when offered. The closer he got, the older the man seemed to be. Myles thought him to be in his late seventies.

"Myles Kramer, homicide detective for this district." Myles introduced himself as they shook. "My officer tells me you might have something to offer on this…case?"

Hooper looked around and then back at Myles. That was when Myles noticed the deep scars in his throat and cheek. Before he could comment on it, Gregory looked him in the eye as if he knew what he was thinking.

"Is there somewhere we can go to talk? I don't…if you don't believe me, I'd rather not have any witnesses again. I've been told I was crazy before and I don't much care for it even after all this time."

Myles nodded and told one of the men milling about to call him on his cell if and when the coroner showed up. The crime scene boys couldn't do a damned thing without someone there to pronounce that the several hundred body parts for the three men and the woman strewn about the room were all dead.

They ended up in a conference room just around the corner from the bar. The hotel was clearing out quickly and Myles really couldn't blame the patrons. Once word started to get out that there was someone killing off the guests, it sort of put a damper on the fun here in the Big Apple.

"I used to work homicide too. Though I wasn't a detective back then. I was just a beat cop who was pulled in to do a little leg work for the big boys." Gregory smiled at Myles as he continued. "We didn't have all this stuff that you boys have now. It was a lot more guess work than anything else."

"We still do a lot of guessing too. Most of the time that's all it is and a lucky break. The cops have gotten a lot smarter, but so have the criminals. More so I think than us if you want to know the truth." Myles looked up as one of the girls that had been in the back room of the bar when everything went hinky walked in. "The desk guy said we can use this room. If it's a problem then we can—"

"No, he said to ask you if you needed anything. He said he'd like you to get this solved quickly and making you happy is our next priority."

Myles looked at Gregory and he shook his head. "Just some water if you don't mind. After you bring it in we'd like to not be disturbed. Police business, you know."

She moved a cart into the room that had been out of his sight. There were two pitchers of water and an assortment of soft drinks, as well as some glasses and ice. Myles didn't know who the guy thought he was serving in here, but the two of them could drink for a month and not drink all this. After the girl left, refusing a tip, Gregory started again.

"I was helping out on this case, you see. It was back awhile when a bunch of bodies showed up. They'd been torn up." The man reached into his jacket pocket and pulled out an envelope. "Mind, we didn't have the cameras there are now to take pictures, but I think you'll see what I did."

Myles opened the envelope and several pictures, all five-by-sevens, spilled out on the conference table. They were all in black and white, but he didn't need color to tell him that it was the same as he had in the bar now.

"Where was this?" He sorted through the pictures and counted three men and one woman. "Did you ever find the killer?"

"Jersey City, and no. They were all in a bar or something similar to it. Nothing much like the one you're in now. Back then there were more witnesses, or I should say more people around. They didn't have anything to tell us. All we got out of them was they were suddenly covered in blood." Gregory, using his finger, pushed a photo of a girl to him. "This here is Theresa. She was the first one that called us. She screamed to the dispatcher that there were a hundred people dead and that she thought maybe about that many people had done the killing."

Myles looked at the girl. She looked to be about twenty, maybe less, but no more than that. Pretty little thing with dark hair and dark eyes. That's all he could tell by the photo. He looked at the back of the picture and read her name and address. It was an address in Jersey City. He put the photo down and looked at Gregory. The man had yet to tell him anything all that helpful, but Myles thought the best was yet to come.

"You want to tell me what it is you're hoping I'll guess? I've got a few murders to solve and so far, all you've told me is that you have a crime similar to mine that happened a long time ago." Myles watched as he pulled out another envelope from the other side of his jacket. "What's this? More ancient pictures?"

The first picture sent a wave of cold air over his body. It was another bar, more dead people, and more blood. These pictures were in color. While Myles looked these over, Gregory stacked the first set of pictures up and told him about this set.

"Those were taken five years later. There were two more like this between the first and those, but the pictures were ruined during a fire in the basement of the station. I heard that the bodies were the same, three men and a woman. Same as the one you have in your hand. I got another two envelopes of pictures if you need to see them, but you'll pretty much see the same thing. Blood, bodies, and three men and one single woman." He put the first pictures back into his pocket. "That is the girl who called it in."

It was the same girl. Her hair was different, lighter than in the first one, and in this one he could see that her eyes were a deep brown. He flipped the picture over. The name was the same too.

"This one says she lives in Hudson district. That's about two hundred miles away. How did you get to be on both crime scenes?" Myles kept staring at the girl so it took him a few minutes to realize that Gregory hadn't answered. "You've been gathering this information since then, haven't you?"

"Yes. After the second killing, I started keeping my own notes and files. It wasn't as hard back then, just ask the clerk at the print job to make you another set. And the newspaper didn't care if I slipped them a few bucks to have anything extra they might have taken." He took out a larger envelope, this time from the back of his jacket. "Those are my notes and anything else I have. I got more in my hotel room here."

"Why?" Myles was going to take it all. If even half of what he was seeing in these pictures were true, then he wanted it all. "And what is the connection to all these deaths other than the girl? Why is she killing them?"

Gregory laughed. "Took me nearly five years to realize she was the killer. She had me fooled with the hair changes. And I suppose the way she didn't age nary a bit." He dumped the last pictures, these glossy color eight-by-tens. "She called in that one about a month ago. I was visiting a friend or I might have missed it. An old buddy of mine called me and told me about it."

The pictures could have been duplicates of the scene from all the others. And the blood and gore seemed to be more...well, simply more. He looked for the girl, knowing there had to be a picture, when he found it. She looked to be exactly the same as she had in the first picture. Myles looked up at Gregory.

"When was the first murder committed? What year?" Myles didn't really want to know, was afraid to know really, but knew that as sure as he was sitting there it had to have been at least twenty or so years ago—maybe as many as thirty.

"I'll be seventy-five on my next birthday. I was eighteen when that first one happened."

Myles sat in the same chair long after Gregory left, leaving him the key to his room. He told Myles that he was leaving as soon as he got in his car and not coming back. He said he wasn't long for this earth, that he'd been a heavy smoker all his life and it had finally caught up with him.

"Cancer got me. I guess I had it better than most, lived myself a long life. Not much of one, mind you, but a long one." Gregory had stood and so did Myles. "You find her for me. Find her and kill her. That's the only way to make sure that nothing like this happens again."

He told him he'd do his best and sat back down at the table to look over the crime scene photos. Whatever this girl was, and he had no doubt that she wasn't quite human, she was one pissed off bitch.

~~~

Theresa watched everything going on with a smile. Humans were so stupid, and she laughed harder when one of the policemen came out and threw up all over the hedge near the hotel. Yes, they were incredibly stupid.

She wanted to move closer but stayed back. She'd learned recently that there were cameras all around, and sometimes they'd catch her in the crowd. Then she thought about her buddy Gregory.

He'd been here. Later, but he'd been here. She could find him by scent now, and sniffed the air to see if he'd been close enough that she could brush by him. Nothing. She did smell something…almost something she liked, but decided it was the scent of blood and dismissed it. It wasn't until she was moving toward her den that she realized what she'd smelled.

Vampire. An old one too. Turning to go back to where she'd been standing, Theresa changed her mind. If she could smell him then he would be able to smell her too. Picking up speed, she made her way to her resting area with five minutes to spare, and wondered if the old one had made it as well. Huddled down into the deepest part of the cave, she thought about what she'd done last evening.

When she'd first entered the bar it hadn't been her intention to kill anyone. She'd only wanted a fast meal, and had happened upon the place because it was open. Going into the bar, she could feel the others there, but not in view of her. She went to the wall where she could hear them but not see them, and listened.

She could hear that they were there to kill a woman who they believed was a hired killer. Intrigued, she slipped into the room where they were using all sorts of equipment she'd only just recently started to pay attention to. She realized that they were listening in on someone. It only took her a few seconds to realize that here was an opportunity she couldn't pass up. But it wasn't until she was actually in the room that she realized she'd miscalculated, and there were only two men in the room with a woman.

Killing the two men had been easy. She simply took the woman to her body and sank her fangs deep into her throat while they watched. She had no idea why some people thought this was incredibly erotic, but they sat long enough for her to feed enough to handle the two of them and drop the woman to the floor. Theresa had the neck of the first man broken before he could even make a sound. The second man was a bit trickier, but he was no match for her strength, and when he stood to attack, finally, she simply moved to him and lifted him off the floor by his neck until he stopped struggling. He was dead before she went back to the woman to finish feeding.

Tearing them apart had been fun. She loved the sounds the body made when it was torn to bits…bones cracking, flesh tearing. She did miss the sounds of them crying and begging for their release, but this hadn't been planned and she was doing the best she could with what she had to work with. It was then that she went to the bar and tore the man up with the other woman, wishing the entire time that she'd waited for his companion, the female with him. She would have been much more fun.

Theresa hadn't been a vampire long when she realized how much fun she could have with her newfound strength. The first time she'd killed had made her climax better than she ever had, even as a human. She'd had to do it again and again for the same thrill, getting better all the time. Smiling, she remembered the first time she'd killed four and found it to be the perfect combination of humans so that she had the optimum fun. Three were nothing but a lot of fun, and five had taken too long and she'd been too exhausted to enjoy the aftermath.

The third time she'd killed her quad was when she'd seen Gregory. He'd been on the case with some other detectives; back then, they'd simply been cops. And he'd been so nice to her when she'd told him what she'd "witnessed" that she'd made sure over the years that he'd get a call either from her or another person she'd made call him so she could see him again. She wished he hadn't gotten old, but it wasn't until recently that she realized she could have changed him into what she was and he would have been around for a lot longer. Now, he was old and dying, and she was getting bored with him.

As the sun started to rise Theresa thought of the scent she'd picked up in the bar and wondered who it had been. She thought that she'd go back there tomorrow, sniff around, and see what she could find. Maybe she'd be able to find whoever it had been in the room by following its trail. Smiling at the prospect of finding the scent, she closed her eyes just as the sun crested the horizon. Theresa was out before the sun was much more than a bright spot in the sky.

CHAPTER 4

Holly woke with the sun streaming through the windows. She couldn't believe that she'd forgotten to close the curtains again and started to get up. She realized several things almost at once.

First, she was naked. That wasn't really a big thing, but on a scale of one to ten on her "what the hell happened last night scale," it rated about a five. The second thing was that she was sore. Sore in places she'd…well, with the naked factor right there, being naked and sore gave her enough of a pause to bring the first score up a notch or two. But what was freaking her the hell out was the huge arm around her waist…the one that was currently pulling her back into the bed and growling at her. Then he spoke.

"I didn't get back in until just a few hours ago. If you go back to sleep now I'll make it worth your while later after I've had another hour sleep."

Her heart started pounding in her chest, and when he slid his very naked leg up and over hers, she nearly swallowed her tongue. But she had to be sure. Closing her eyes so she could think without screaming, she turned slightly before speaking.

"Phil?" He growled again. "Phil, what the hell are you doing in my bed and where...oh my fucking—we had sex." She started to pull away again.

"Yes, we did. And, if you're a good girl, we'll have it a lot more. Just not right now. I went back to the bar to see if I could figure out what it was that—"

She leapt from the bed and then jumped back when she remembered her lack of attire. "Where are my clothes? We can't be...what are you doing here? And the bar? I don't remember meeting you for—"

Then it hit her. Not in a gentle, bits and pieces, sort of slow move through her brain, but a full on assault. Blood and her target. The arm that had landed only inches from where she sat. Phil taking her to this room quickly, so quickly that she'd buried her face in his neck so that she wouldn't get sick seeing everything blur by them. She pulled the blanket up over her head and waited for something, anything, to tell her it was a dream.

"It wasn't. A dream. Those people were killed by.... Holly, honey, please don't cry." She hadn't realized she had been until he'd said it. "Come on, sweetheart, let me hold you. It'll be all right. I've got you now."

"How will it be all right? Did they catch that...that thing that did that to them? Oh Phil, those poor people. What did that to them?" She wrapped herself around him when he pulled her closer. "I was sitting right there. I could have been kil—"

"No. Don't think like that. You were there, but the person had already killed a woman and you were not what it was looking for anyway. She...I think it was the female that the police were talking about."

She looked up at him when he stopped talking.

"What female? You talked to the police? Oh shit, do they know who I am? I have to get out of here. I can't be caught here." He pulled her back to him again when she started to get up. "You don't understand. I can't be caught. The government will not only let me rot in prison, but will more than likely have me murdered to keep me quiet."

"You're not going anywhere. I want you to tell me what you knew of those people down there. The police have figured out they were all there together and will begin to ask questions about them soon." He cleared his throat before he continued. "I listened in on a conversation enough to know that this person, a woman they are calling Theresa Doe, is who they believe is responsible. She's been killing people, always in fours, for decades."

She laid back and tried to ignore the fact that he was hard beside her. His quick "behave" had her trying to think of anything but him, but it only made her think of him more. When he groaned, she looked up at him.

"You can't expect me to lay here beside you while your scent is calling to me. Either think of something else or we'll be having this conversation much later." He rocked into her hip and she couldn't help but moan. "Christ, I want you."

She pulled him over her and wrapped her arms around his neck. There was nothing between them now since she'd gotten up, and when he brushed his hairy chest over hers to kiss her, her nipples peaked when he touched her. Bringing her hands up his waist to his chest, she flicked his nipple with her nail. Bolder now that she could make him growl, she did it again.

Shifting on the bed, she moved so that she could lick his chest. Nothing had prepared her for the taste, and she doubted that if she licked every man in the world she'd ever find anything that tasted quite so delicious. When she took the hard peak into her mouth and nipped, he wrapped his hand into her hair and pulled her back.

"I want more. Let me have my fill of you." She pulled away from him slowly and grinned as she rolled him to his back and straddled him. "I can touch you this way. All of you until my heart's content."

He put his hands on her hips, and all she could think about was the way he'd done the same thing last night on the cold floor. Moving back on his hips, she could feel his stiff cock at her ass and thought about how much he'd filled her with it.

"Holly, you're killing me. I need to be inside of you again. Or better yet, move up here and let me lick you this way. Move that pretty little pussy over my mouth and let me fuck you with my tongue." She decided that he had a wonderful idea. "Hold onto the headboard and get up on your knees for me. That's it, baby."

When she looked down between her thighs she could see him there. His mouth was moving up her leg toward her pussy, slowly nibbling as he went. When he pulled her hips down she let him, and cried out when he suckled her clit into his mouth.

She gripped the frame in her hand as she rode his mouth. When she felt his finger move along her slit she widened her position for him and moaned when he was deep inside of her. Then when she felt his finger at her ass, she slowed her dance over his mouth until he pulled away and looked up at her.

"I won't hurt you. I swear it. I want to give you as much pleasure as I possibly can before I fuck you. Coming now will loosen you up for my cock and I don't want to hurt you again." She nodded when he moved at her tight hole. When his finger slid in, she nearly came up off the bed, not from pain but from the most incredible pleasure she'd ever felt.

"You liked that, didn't you? My finger fucking you while you ride my mouth. Good. Give me your pussy, baby. I'm going to make you come hard like this." She moved back to his mouth as he moved slowly inside of her. Dark pleasure rode over her and she could feel her pussy flood with pleasure. Soon she was riding him faster and harder, ready for the climax that was building as fast as Phil was fucking her.

It didn't just come over her but pounded her from every fiber in her body. Screaming out his name, she threw back her head and let go of the frame she'd been clinging to. The first time her hand brushed over her nipple, she filled her hands with both of her breasts and squeezed hard, pinching her nipples and rolling them tight between her thumbs and fingers. When she felt the bed at her back she instinctively opened her legs and let him slide into her. His cock filled her fully and she could taste herself on his mouth when he devoured her.

Need, a need like she'd never felt, hit her. She wanted to bite him, take his flesh into her mouth and bite him hard enough to taste his blood, take it into her body. When his tongue slid along her throat, her canines dropped and she knew that she had to mark him. Licking his shoulder, she felt his fangs scrape along her vein just as she was preparing to bite him. When he roared out his release she came too, sank her teeth deep into his muscle, and knew that he'd bitten her as well.

~~~

Phil didn't move. He wanted to, he was sure that he was heavy over her, but didn't want to move in the event that she was pissed. They'd bonded now, at least enough that she was his mate and he hers. There was still the ceremonial bonding for them both, hers in front of her pack and his with his family dagger.

When she stirred he lifted his head and looked down at her. Christ, she was beautiful.

"I guess we've taken the final steps to be one." She looked away and he brought her face back so that he could see her as she continued. "Are you upset with me?"

"No. Why would I be? I've been in love with you since I saw you kick your brother's ass on the sidewalk in front of my office ten years ago." He grinned when she did. "You have a vicious way of making a point."

"Connor. He'd been dating one of my friends and he was dumping her because she told him she was looking for more out of their relationship. I hadn't understood the way we were bonded to one person and that was all there was. Well, I understood, I just didn't want to see my friend hurt." She shifted her body so that she was no longer under him, but she made no move to get up. "We probably should have talked a bit more before leaping into this. You don't...I'm not a good person. I kill people for a living and I don't know how you feel about that."

He wasn't thrilled about her job, but knew better than to tell her she was going to stop doing it. He'd seen enough relationships, both human and not, to know that a couple agreed about things...one did not order the other about as if they were stupid. Phil moved her hair from her throat and ran the pad of his thumb up the pulse beating there. She shivered and he smiled.

"I think we need to talk about it, but as for you not being a good person? That's not even close to the truth. You're the most wonderful person I know. You're my mate, how could you be anything less than that?" He rolled to his back and took her with him. He loved the feel of her warm body spread over his. "I think you should tell me what you do and who you work for now. And I'll tell you what I know about what happened downstairs."

"I work for a branch of the government that I'm not sure has a title. If they do, it's buried so deep in paperwork that I doubt even any of them know it. But I started working for them right out of high school. I'd taken those aptitude tests they give you and scored very high." She lifted her head and rested it on her fist on his chest. "I have a contact that sends me a folder when I need to contact them. There is a phone and a sheet of paper that has only a time on it. Whoever it is calls me at that time."

"Then that's how they tell you what to do? Seems risky giving that out over a cell phone." He frowned when she shook her head. "Then what? Please don't tell me you meet them somewhere."

"Yes. But it's all very clandestine. It's a meeting in several places. Twenty minutes in one place, ten in another, until we get all the information traded that I need. And anything extra I have to use is bought by me with my own money and they send the reimbursement to a bank account that only I can get into." He doubted that, but she continued with her story. "Basically, I have a time frame in which to work, what they need from my end, and a picture. They get their information the same way I get mine."

"Not that it's any of my business, but—"

"Yes, it is. Everything is." She flushed. "I'm sorry. I don't want to fight with you all the time like CJ and Austin did. But I don't want you to make me feel like I'm stupid either."

He pulled her to his mouth and kissed her. "Never. And I was thinking the same thing. At least this time with your family you don't have to have me prove what we are. I'm pretty sure you get it." He laughed again. "I'm so in love with you, Holly."

"I guess I love you too." This time when she flushed he squeezed her tighter. "What were you going to ask me?"

He let her change the subject. He wasn't happy about the "guessing" she loved him part, but he could understand her hesitancy too. He did have to think a bit about what he'd been about to ask her, and decided that how she got paid really wasn't any of his business other than he was worried about her. So he asked.

"They send me a check for some of it. It's under the heading of this fake storefront in Ohio that my family thinks I work for. The rest goes into a safety deposit box that I go to when I feel like." That bothered him too. The fact that anyone who knew where the account was could get to her by simply watching the bank made him think that she was going to be hurt if at any time they decided that she was no longer an asset to them.

Her belly growled and he laughed at her. She told him she was hungry and that, unlike him, she needed to eat more just to keep her body in tiptop shape. That stopped him in his move to get up. Rolling her back to the bed, he covered her with his body and rocked his cock hard between her legs. Watching her face, he slowly entered her, sliding his cock deep.

"If your body got any better I'd be a dead man." His balls tightened up close to his body as he felt his climax coming fast. "Holly, drink from me. I want to feel your every thought, every need. Please, drink from me."

She took his wrist to her mouth and licked him. He knew that she couldn't bite him without hurting him so he took his wrist back and bit deep for her as he moved his cock in and out of her. As soon as he put her mouth to his wound, she wrapped her legs around his thighs and surged up with every one of his downward strokes. When she suckled, drank from him, he came. Then as she came around him, he felt his cock fill again and he jettisoned into her, filling her with his seed.

Christ, they were going to kill each other if they kept this up. He pulled her body over his again and he heard her soft snore. So much for breakfast, he thought with a grin. Looking over at this watch, he saw that it was just after ten in the morning. Thinking that they'd sleep for a little while, he closed his eyes. Later…later they'd talk about the woman and what she was doing to the humans in the world.

CHAPTER 5

Austin looked over at his mate. The way she was moving made him think that she should have stayed at home. She was miserable and he was terrified for her. Being near her term, everything made him think she was going to deliver at any second. He was sure they were going to have their pup in the airport waiting for his sister and her mate. He tried to smile when CJ glared at him.

"I swear to you the next time you want to have a baby you're the one who is going to carry it. I'm so sick of having you look at me like I'm going to break that I want to get a knife and cut your dick off." She didn't even grin when she said it, so he knew that he had to tread lightly here or she'd follow through on her threat.

"I was just thinking about how beautiful you looked. Even in this heat you look as fresh as a daisy." He knew he'd gone too far when she crossed her arms over her ample belly and tapped her foot. "What? A man can't tell his mate that she looks lovely carrying his child?"

"Not when he says it with a frown marring his forehead. Nor when you know damn good and well that you think I look like a side of a house and waddle like a large, overstuffed penguin."

He snapped his mouth closed, knowing that anything he said now would not only get him hurt, but maybe killed too. He was beginning to think that his brother was right when Dallas told him that he thought pregnancy wasn't for everyone. CJ was definitely not the picture he'd had in mind of someone carrying his child.

"Have nothing to say, big boy? Well, that's probably the smartest thing you've ever done." She glared at a woman making noises about the beauty of pregnant women. "When is his stupid plane supposed to land anyway? I need a nap."

Phil had called him not ten minutes ago and said they were on the tarmac, but he didn't tell her that he'd already told her. He simply said he thought he was already there. Austin was going to do what his mother had told him to do…tread lightly and keep agreeing with everything she said, and never, ever mention the labor and delivery part of this baby. That had nearly cost him his nuts and his ear. He thought at first it had been something the two of them had worked up, but now he could see the wisdom of the advice.

When he saw his sister coming toward them from the gate he could tell something was different. He knew that she and Phil had become mates, not fully yet, but they had started the process. He wasn't sure he liked the idea of his baby sister having sex, but knew that if he even mentioned that, someone, if not all of them, might do something to him. For an alpha, he was having a hard time staying in one piece, and not by anyone but his own family.

"Wow," Holly said when she stepped back after hugging CJ. "You're lovely. I think having babies suits you very well."

Austin waited for the fireworks, a gun to be pulled, or a she-bitch fight to begin, but all CJ did was blush and tell her she'd never felt better. He nearly said, "What the fuck?" but wisely kept his mouth shut. He did look over at Phil, who looked horrified.

"She's due soon. Well, yesterday as a matter of fact. We should be getting back." He was babbling because he was afraid that Phil, for all his age and friendship toward CJ, was going to say something that would get him killed too. "We have to stop by the pack house, then by the doctor's office to sign some papers."

"Do you know what you're having?" Phil asked suddenly. "I mean, have you had any sort of idea what the sex of the baby is yet?"

He looked at Austin when CJ shook her head. Before he could tell him that they'd decided to wait even though he and CJ had thought it was a girl, CJ spoke up.

"I don't want to have someone tell me then they end up being wrong. I want a boy, really badly. A son for Austin." She looked up at him and he could see the tears in her eyes. "I know I've been a real bitch, but I really do want a son for you."

Phil nodded and then took her hand. CJ hugged him to her and Phil winked at him over her shoulder. "Would you like to know for sure? I can tell you both right now if you want to know."

Austin didn't move. They were standing in a busy airport with people moving all around him, and all he could think about was a son. He looked at CJ when he realized she hadn't answered him either. He was so not making this decision without her input first.

"Can you tell one hundred percent what we're having, and not just a guess like the doctor? I know he had one of those internal monitors, but the baby wasn't cooperating with him so he couldn't tell, and now I'm just a bit too far along for them to do another one." CJ looked at Austin before she continued. "Do you want to know? I do if you do."

He nodded. It was about all he could manage right now. Phil put his hands on CJ's belly and closed his eyes. His smile told them nothing and when he stepped back, Austin decided that the next time he had the opportunity he was going to pound his friend into the dirt.

"You're having one of each. The boy is head down and the girl is in the right position. Would you like to know what they think of you?" CJ nodded. "They think they are the luckiest babies in the entire world to have people like you as their parents. And the girl, she's nearly all wolf, the boy is full-blooded."

Austin grabbed the back of the chair he was standing next to. He realized that his sister was speaking to him, but for the life of him he couldn't tell what she was saying. Twins…twins that already loved them.

Austin was suddenly sitting down and he could see the floor from his new position…his head between his knees. He started to rise but was pushed back down again.

"I'm fine. What the hell did you shove me here for, you moronic dick? Let me up I said." He knew that Phil held him down; he could see his shoes in his line of site. "Phil, so help me, when I get up from here, I'm going to shift and tear you apart."

Austin was suddenly free. He didn't stand, not sure his knees would hold him just yet. For all his bravado, he was still a little stunned about twins. He reached for CJ, pulled her to him, and rested his head on her belly. The first kick he got in the cheek made him laugh, the second made him kiss her belly.

"Okay, big boy. If you stop on your way home to get me a glass of tea I'll let you in on a little secret." CJ wiggled her brows at him. "And if you're really nice and get me one that isn't sweetened, I'll give you two."

Austin looked over at Phil, who was frowning again. He wasn't sure what the man had to be upset about…he wasn't the one living with the moodiest woman in the world. He looked back at CJ, ready to give her whatever she wanted, when he noticed she was sweating. Profusely.

"How long have you been in labor, love?" Phil asked her. "I would say you're what…having them about three minutes apart?"

Austin didn't know what he was talking about until Holly spoke. "Oh Christ, you're in labor? Now?"

CJ nodded and grabbed for the chair next to her. "I didn't think it was real. They told me at the doctor's office to expect to have a few dry runs, but these pains, they hurt like hell."

Austin stared at her. He had to have missed something. He looked at Phil when he put his arm around CJ and started moving her toward the door. Quickly. It wasn't until Holly hit him in the head with her purse that he realized something was going on.

"Wake up, you fuck-tard, and get going. You want her to deliver those babies without you?" He stood and stared after Phil and CJ. They were nearly to the door already. Holly hit him again and that's when it sank in.

"Fuck. She's in labor. I have to…where did they go?" Instead of answering him, Holly guided him after them. His mind was suddenly mush. "Where are they going?"

"To the car." He wasn't sure he liked her tone. Sort of a cross between her talking to him like he was four and afraid he was going to fall apart.

"I know that. I was…I was simply testing you." She nodded, but again her body language led him to believe she was humoring him. They made it to the car, which was parked on the sidewalk in front of the doors. He was shoved in the back with CJ.

Austin was being handed out of the car before he could think. The guy standing there had a wheel chair, and Austin started to tell him he was fine now when he was pushed out of the way and the man reached in for CJ. Before he could help, she was being rushed into the hospital doors and away from him again.

"Are you going to be this dense when the pups are born? If so, let me know now so I can get them cell phones with GPS on them. That way when you leave them somewhere, I'll be able to track them down with it." Austin growled at Phil. "You know, you really should get in there, alpha. Your cubs are about to be born."

That got him moving. He heard someone say his name and before he could slow and see what they wanted, Phil was there. He wondered briefly what he'd said to the nurse, but she simply sat back down and resumed working. The three of them rushed to the elevators.

~~~

Phil watched the others in the room. Gordon paced, worried, he was sure, about his own mate, Alexis, who was just beginning to look ready to pop with her pregnancy. Connor sat in the corner and talked with Gordon and Alexis's two boys, Tim and Jake. Darcy and Sis sat and colored in the books that one of the nurses had given them. The four children weren't really Gordon's children and only Alexis's nieces and nephews, but one couldn't tell by looking at them. And they all called them Mom and Dad. The adoption was ready to be finalized any day now.

Nancy Force sat quietly with her eyes closed, but he'd bet all his money that she knew where every one of the people in the room were. She even smiled once in a while, he was sure at something one of the children said.

But Dallas looked upset. Phil had had a few minutes earlier, before everyone had shown up, to give him a heads up on the woman Theresa and her bloody mess and murder at the bar in New York. He didn't mention Holly's involvement, as the two of them had agreed to her telling her family what she did when everyone was all together. Even with them all here, he knew that it would be much later before they got to have a family meeting.

When Austin came through the double doors two hours later, he looked as strange as he'd ever seen him. Walking toward him, Phil was suddenly nervous. The man looked like he was going to first kill him, then eat him for dinner. When he wrapped both his beefy arms around him and almost squeezed the life out of him, Phil nearly passed out.

"Hey there, killer. Want to let me breathe a bit?" Austin let him go for a few seconds only to pull him back in and hug him tighter. "You're happy, I get it, but I have to breathe."

"They're beautiful. And just like you said. My son first then my daughter. They're…I can't tell you how much I already love them." Phil had an idea, but wasn't breathing well yet, so only grunted. "You have to come see them."

They all moved after the two of them. Phil tried in vain to pull his arm free of the giant man, but Austin seemed determined to be in the lead. It wasn't until they were standing before a large glassed-in room that he could see where they'd been going. And right there in the front were two babies with the name "Force" written in a bold hand. Christ, they were beautiful too.

"That one is my son, Austin Jackson Force, and our daughter, Nancy Alexis Force." He pointed to the pink little bundle next to the other one in blue. "She is going to be a daddy's little girl."

Holly snorted and then grinned when Austin glared at her. "You tried that crap on me and it didn't stick. What makes you think I'm going to let her be a girly girl; or, for that matter, her mother let her be a girly girl? CJ is the coolest woman I know and she drives a big rig. That little girl is going to be as tough as nails and meaner than a snake. I'm going to make sure of it."

Phil stepped back and then walked to the elevator. When Holly started to follow he told her he'd be right back. He wanted to go and get something from the gift shop. She said she did as well and they both went down. He looked over at her when she cleared her throat.

"Did you want kids, Phil? Ever?" She looked so sad that he nearly pulled her into his arms, but didn't right away. "My job...I'm pretty sure when I try to quit, they aren't going to throw me a retirement party unless it's of the permanent kind. I don't think I've ever known anyone to give notice with this group and not die of a natural or not so natural cause later."

He nodded, glad that she understood too. "They won't hurt you. Ever. Not so long as I'm around. I swear to you, Holly."

She moved to him and he pulled her close even as the elevator came to a stop. "They don't know what I am. I never told them. I never told anyone what I am. I let them think all this time that I'm super smart and know all there is to know about tracking. They don't have a clue that I shift and hunt my target down by scent as a wolf."

He had already figured out that she did that. He nodded over her head and watched the door open. He shoved her behind him when he saw who was standing there. Phil bowed before the two women and the man and, before he could stand, they spoke as one.

"The council needs you. You will come with us now, Knight of the Order." He rose slowly as the man stepped forward. "There is a problem and you have been—"

"You've a mate. A she-wolf." The darker of the two women spoke alone this time as she sniffed the air. "She will be required as well."

When they touched him he could feel the air rushing around them, and knew that there was nothing at all he could do other than hope that Holly was all right. Phil hadn't seen this group of warriors since just after his two hundredth year.

When they stopped suddenly he reached for Holly. He knew she'd be sick. He had been the first time he'd traveled this way. But she wasn't. If anything, she looked more beautiful than he'd ever seen her, and she was pissed. He didn't even try to hold her back knowing that as his mate, they would never dare to harm her.

"You take us back right fucking now. My brother and my best friend just had their first cubs and you pulling this shit on us before I get the chance to hold either of them is bullshit." She put her hands on her hips and started to tap her foot. "Well, I don't see any of you rushing to do what I said. I can only conclude that you're either incredibly stupid, deaf, or you want to make me get all medieval on your asses."

Phil couldn't help it; he threw back his head and laughed. He'd never seen anyone with more confused looks on their faces than the men and women assembled before them. He took Holly's hand and kissed the back of it before he addressed them formally.

"Council, My Lady, I'd like to present my mate to you, Holly Force Campbell. Holly, this is Anye Sabalz and the High Trustees of Vampires. Anye is the head of this smaller group of council members and the one who decides everything." He bowed before them and was happy to see Holly do the same. "Council."

"We have a rogue. She is…we believe that she may catch your scent and will now follow you back to your home. There will be trouble for all those that you have taken to your heart if she succeeds in finding you," Anye said without any preamble. "If she makes it to the area, she will need to be taken down. We ask you for your help once again, Knight Campbell."

He bowed again. "And would her name be Theresa Sykes?"

CHAPTER 6

Holly was still thinking about the fact that Phil was a knight when they were brought back to their realm. She didn't know what to say to him and wasn't sure what she wanted to ask him either. They were buying nearly every toy in the gift shop when she suddenly sat down on the floor.

"Holly, are you all right?" She didn't know how to answer that, so she didn't. "Holly, you're scaring the nice people in here. Is this after effects of the trip? I assure you that when we have to travel like that again, you won't even feel it. The first time is always the hardest."

"We will be traveling that way again?" she asked him incredulously. It was suddenly too much and she needed some air. "I'll be back. Don't follow me."

She threw everything she had in her arms at the startled girl at the counter and was out the door and into the hot afternoon sun. Looking up at the sky, she took several deep breaths when she felt him stirring in her mind.

I won't follow you if you please tell me what's wrong. Is it because I have to go and find this woman? I assure you, if I had a choice, I'd rather stay home with you and make love all night.

Sighing heavily, she sat down on the bench before answering him the same way. No. It's just that…were you going to tell me about your knighthood? I mean, that seems like a really big deal. And the fact that they nearly fell all over themselves trying to please you was sort of disconcerting. Especially since I kind of thought you worked for them.

I do, work for them I mean. And, yes, they want to please me. Very badly. They can't make me do what they want and if I say no, they have no one else. She felt his distraction and knew he was paying for the gifts and talking to the girl about all of it. Remind me never to take you shopping again. I think spending three thousand dollars on two infants that can't even play with these things is a little extravagant, don't you?

There are things in there for the other children too, and also CJ. And don't change the subject. When were you going to tell me about being a knight? She felt his laughter and knew that he was laughing at her. Behave or I'll sleep on the couch tonight.

Highly doubtful, love, since I can feel your arousal. She felt him move over her body almost as if he were standing right next to her, and her nipples pebbled in her bra. Hum, I can almost taste you on my tongue still. I love lapping at your cream while you ride my face.

Stop that and answer me. She had to shift on the bench twice before she thought she could breathe correctly. If I have to hunt you down you're not going to be a very happy vamp.

I was knighted just after I hit my one hundredth year. I was…working for them at the time and they decided to reward me for something I did. He paused before continuing. Are you coming back inside to help me carry this stuff up to CJ's room?

She knew that as far as he was concerned the subject was closed. She stood up and grinned. Far from it, she thought, as she made her way back to the hospital entrance. Very far from it.

By the time she caught up with him, he was standing in front of the elevators. She took the large, stuffed pink bear and left him with the large blue dog. There were still several bags in his hands and she took two of them.

"I guess we did go a little overboard. But CJ is my friend as well as my sister-in-law." He kissed her quickly on the mouth as she tried to explain to him. "Well, you did buy some of this."

"So I did. And frankly, I don't care how much we spend on everyone. I'm in too good a mood to let a little money bother me. I have far more than I need or will ever spend, and I'm going to have a little fun with it." He set down the blue dog and reached into his pocket. "I bought this for you. It's temporary. We'll get us a better one when we can get somewhere to pick it out."

She opened the small bag and squealed in delight at the little ring inside. It was perfect. A small band was surrounded in wolves chasing each other round and round it. She was about to slip it on her finger when he told her to wait. Going down on one knee, he took the ring from her and kissed her finger before sliding it over the first knuckle.

"I love you with all my heart and will always do so. There is nothing I'd like more than to spend all eternity with you at my side. Holly Force, will you be my vampire bride?" He wiggled his brows at her and made her giggle. "I love you, will you marry me?"

The doors slid open just as she answered him. Dallas, of course, had to hold the door open while he pulled nearly every person he saw into the tiny space to meet his sister, who was getting married. By the time they made it back to CJ's room they'd been hugged, congratulated, and kissed by everyone.

She was still wiping her cheeks from all the kisses when she entered the room.

"Let me see it," CJ said from her perch on the bed. Holly ran over and let her look at the ring while Austin and the rest of her brothers threatened Phil with every kind of injury if he hurt her. He told them he was more afraid of her hurting him than the other way around. By the time they left the room and all the gifts had been ahhed over, CJ was dozing and Austin looked ready to drop.

"I'd like to set up a meeting with you and Austin tomorrow," Phil told Dallas when they walked to the parking garage. "There are some things that have happened that you and the pack need to be made aware of."

"And I have something to tell you as well. Something that I should have told you a long time ago." She could tell that Connor wanted to make a joke, but a small shake of her head had him stopping. "It's really important that we all are there with this."

Dallas looked concerned, but he agreed. "They are going to let CJ come home tomorrow. The pups are fine and the doctor knows we'll be taking care of her well enough. I don't suppose you can give me a hint, something that I can think about rather than all the horrible things that are currently running through my head right now?"

Holly looked at Phil and waited. She had expected this and so, apparently, had Phil. He handed a file to Dallas, part of the one he'd been given by Anye, asking that he keep this between the two of them until they all talked. He agreed.

"But I'll need to tell Austin what I know. He's not only my brother, but my alpha as well. I can't...no, I won't keep secrets from him. Especially if it concerns my entire family."

Holly felt her pride in her brother go up another notch. He was the best man for a job like this. Keeping a secret like this could and would get a few people killed if the wrong information got out. Then there was her whole sordid tale. They all agreed to meet at the pack house for dinner.

They were driving back when she thought of something else. "How did you know who the woman was when Anye said she had a rogue? You seemed to already have a really good idea about her before we were summoned."

"Summoned. I suppose that's as good a word for what they did as any other." He parked the car alongside of the road and turned to her in the seat. "How much do you know about my kind? Other than what you've read in books that have never gotten it right."

"Not much, I suppose. I did look up a bit after I...after I figured out what you were to me. But it was less than helpful. Some of the information was so screwed up that I ended up tossing it away." She looked at him and frowned. "Why? What is it I need to know?"

"I would like to say everything, but I know that would only frustrate you and me too. But you should know a few things. Firstly, I'm not a full-blooded vampire. My mother is, but my dad isn't. He was converted when they fell in love. I should also point out that I have...powers, or magic that most vampires, full or not, don't ever achieve."

She waited for him to continue, but he sat there staring at her. She reached for his hand and he held it. "What else should I know? You don't want to tell me, but I'd really like to know."

"One of my powers is the gift of longevity. It doesn't make you immortal, not until I convert you, but you can live a lot longer than the average person, or wolf in this case." She knew she wasn't going to like where this was going, but he continued before she could tell him to stop. "I've given it to your family, all but your mom. She wouldn't let me."

55

"Why? Wait, don't tell me. She said she wanted to join Dad, didn't she? I can see her doing that." Holly nodded. "Yes, I can see that. She really misses him a great deal."

He laughed. "And you're all right with this? I thought you'd demand that I give it to her anyway. I thought for sure you'd say, 'to hell with Dad,' or some other bullshit like that."

"No. I know how much Mom loved Dad. I think she always will. She has told us all on many occasions that she only stayed for all of us. That she loved us all, but she really missed him." Holly looked at Phil and wondered if she and he could have that sort of love. "What else did you need for me to know?"

"I can make people believe what I need them to. Such as the two men who were discussing the murders in the hotel bar. I had them believe they were the only two people in that room, even though I sat next to them the entire time. The older man, Gregory Hooper, has had dealings with the murderer before." He pulled another envelope out of his jacket pocket. "Gregory told the cop, a homicide detective named Myles Kramer, that he had some information on the woman, the murderer in his room. I went up before the cop did and looked around. I even managed to make a few copies of some of the stuff he had."

She took the envelope and opened it. The picture of the woman didn't look familiar. She was a pretty little thing and Holly thought her too young and much too small to have done the damage that she'd done to the people in the bar. She looked up at Phil suddenly.

"She's the rogue." He nodded as she looked back down at the other pictures. "You said this guy—Hooper—you said he had had dealings with her before. How?"

"He was a runner for the cops at one time. When the call came in, he'd go for the experience and for the extra cash. He would pound the pavement or knock on doors to gather information then take it back to the cop in charge. He was young the first time he happened on the crime scene with his fellow officers." She didn't care for the way he'd said young.

"Are you telling me he's not young now? How long…Christ, how long has it been? Years, decades? What?"

"Yes," he said. "Decades. He had been gathering information for nearly sixty years." Phil took out a sheet of paper from the envelope and handed it to her. "I found this on the back of one of his sheets of notes. I think it's her. I think she has been making sure he's been there for each of her killings to…I don't know, taunt him."

"'Next time where the gren tye. Its prety on your eyes. TES'"

Holly read it three times before she looked at Phil. "She isn't educated. And her printing tells me that she didn't finish a grade that would have let her learn cursive. From the picture, I'd say she has had some training in hygiene but very little. And I would bet she cuts her own hair." She looked up at him when he laughed. "What?"

"Nothing. What else do you see there? There is much more if you look at it. And by the way, I'd not caught the hair cutting. Thank you for that."

She felt both stupid and prideful at his words. She looked down at the sheet again. "Is this the original?"

"No. I couldn't take that. It might have held clues that I can't glean from it. But it is a very good copy of his notes about her and her note to him." She flipped the paper over as he continued. "See the name of the hotel? That's where she committed the murders, I'm betting, and he used the hotel stationary to make notes at the scene. The second sheet,"—he handed her this one too—"it has a crude drawing on it. See where he has it marked with the body parts?"

She nodded, and when he told her to buckle up, he was taking them to the house, she did so without putting the notes away. She knew they were missing something and knew that it was staring right at them. She turned the paper over to her note again.

"You called her Theresa, but she signed her name 'Tes.' Why is that? Tes isn't short for Theresa is it?"

"I don't know," he answered with a frown. "Maybe she couldn't spell her name and that was the best she could do."

"No, that's not right. Every child can spell his or her name. It's one of the first things our mom taught us." She kept looking at it even as Phil unloaded the car and took their things into his house. It never occurred to her to protest. They were mates and this was where she belonged.

"Maybe it's not her name at all. Maybe it's her initials. See? It says 'TES,' not Tess with two Ss." He took the paper from her and handed it back without saying anything. She wasn't hurt, she knew he was thinking. She went to the refrigerator and starting taking out the stuff to make dinner. There were two thick steaks on a platter with plastic over it. She held them out to him with a cocked brow.

"I had the cook put them out. I wasn't sure you'd be hungry, but I wanted to have something that you could...I wanted you to be able to...."

"Replenish my blood? Good thinking." She turned away before he could see her smile. "I don't want to get sick before I have to move all my things back to my apartment in a few hours."

His low growl was all the warning she had before he had her sitting on the counter and him between her legs. She smiled at him as she wrapped her arms around his neck.

"You're not a very nice person. I should spank you for teasing me." She licked his nose at his threat. "Yes, that's very nice, but I have something else you can lick. I'm pretty sure the steaks will wait for a—"

His cell phone ringing stopped him. She grinned when he said, "Hello, Mom," and walked away from her. She hopped off the counter and started to put together potatoes for baking and a nice salad. She had the spuds in the oven and the salad nearly made when he closed his phone. He didn't look all that happy.

"My parents are coming to visit. They want to get to know you a lot better. I tried to tell them to wait, but they insisted they could help us." He sat down and put his forehead on the table. "I so don't need this right now."

She was still laughing when, an hour later, two very beautiful people were standing in the kitchen with them. The man looked like Phil—or she supposed Phil looked like him— and the woman was simply beautiful. She took the salad bowl from her as she started to clear the table and handed it to Phil.

"Welcome to the family, dear. Now, tell us what is going on that Phillip doesn't want his parents hanging around for?"

Yep, Holly liked his mom just that quick.

CHAPTER 7

Theresa walked through the bar, ignoring the police tape. She sniffed the air every few minutes, hoping for the other scent again. There were others there…she'd found the older vamp and where he was staying, but she'd never been able to figure out the other scent. It was female, of course, but what kind she couldn't seem to get. Theresa sat in the seat where the other woman had sat.

The smell of the other vampire was on the seat too, like he'd been there as well or had touched the other female. Theresa didn't know why that bothered her, but it did. Pissed her off, if she was truthful with herself.

Theresa looked around the room from there. The bar was right in front of her, as well as the chair where the other man had sat. She'd wanted to kill him, the other one listening in, but had her men already counted for. Theresa could also see where the vamp had sat and thought maybe they'd known each other. Getting up, she went to the hotel front desk.

As computers hadn't been around when she'd been made she didn't understand them, but she did have the ability to make the clerk standing there do almost everything she needed. Theresa still had trouble making anyone do exactly

61

what she needed, and it usually ended up entirely wrong. But this time, she was able to get the girl to see who had stayed in the room she'd followed the vamp up to. Phil Campbell, attorney at law, and it said he lived in Ohio.

Theresa was still looking over his information when the clerk, Debi, said something that had Theresa looking up more information.

"Oh, the pretty couple," she had told the man standing next to her as she pointed to the screen. "Do you think Miss Force and Mr. Campbell got married like he said they were?"

Theresa walked away from the counter twenty-five frustrating minutes later a very happy person. Not only did she have Phil's name, but that of the other woman…Holly P. Force, buyer. Theresa glanced back at the mess she'd left there. Too bad she'd had to kill them both. Laughing, she shook her head. No, it wasn't. Smiling she realized she'd enjoyed every second of their dying.

Theresa had to steal three wallets and two purses before she found enough cash to buy a plane ticket. A horrible fear of flying had her hiding in the bathroom all the way from New York to Ohio. Twice she snarled at a couple of people when they'd tried to open the door with a key, and had giggled a little when they'd complained that someone was going to be in big trouble for bringing their mean dog on board. Theresa rushed out of the tiny room and was out of the plane before they had the chance to put out a means for everyone else to get off.

Not that she cared. To her way of thinking, flying should be left for the birds and if it hadn't been for the fact that she wanted to get to the man and woman before her next killing quota, she would have taken a car. She really did love to drive. Pulling out a phone book, one smaller than she'd thought it should be for a city as big as Columbus, she looked up her attorney's name. He wasn't listed.

Pissed, hungry, and the sun nearly coming up, Theresa took her dinner to a cave with her. The woman hadn't fought her much and when Theresa sank her fangs into her neck, she realized why. Drugs. And lots of them. Not only that, but the woman had a disease; something that Theresa didn't know, but whatever it was made her blood bitter. She drank only what she needed and left the whore to die. She was nearly there anyway; Theresa just helped her along a little bit.

She was settling down in the deepest part of the cave when she remembered becoming a vampire. Theresa had only been sixteen when she'd met her true love. He'd been so nice to her at the church picnic one Sunday that she'd allowed him to kiss her on the cheek before she'd gone home with her daddy.

Her momma had died when she'd been born. Her father had always told her it wasn't her fault that her momma had died birthing her, but she'd never been able to shake the feeling that he did sort of blame her. She'd see the way he'd look at her sometimes, as if he wanted her dead too.

Then the next afternoon the boy, Ernie Richardson, had come calling. She'd blushed horribly at that. Her daddy hadn't been all that happy about it, but he'd allowed them to sit on the porch together for a spell. Her great-aunt Sadie had put up a fuss, but her daddy had let her sit with Mr. Richardson for a whole hour before he'd made him leave.

"I'd like to come tomorrow too if you'll allow it, sir. I really like your daughter and want to get to know her better, if you don't mind." Mr. Richardson had stood there, all tall and beautiful, and when her daddy had looked over at her, she'd nodded.

"You can come, but you should know that she ain't very smart. Couldn't get her to go and finish up her schooling. Got to the third grade and all, but nothing would make her go anymore."

Theresa stared at her daddy for saying such a thing. It was true, but he shouldn't have said it to her new beau.

Mr. Richardson nodded. "Yes, sir. I don't mind that she's dumb. I'll be needing to take me a wife soon and she is about the prettiest thing in this here county. Miss Theresa will suit me, I think."

Long after Mr. Richardson left she still sat on the porch and wondered if he'd insulted her or not. She'd been called stupid before and not just by her daddy, but this time it hurt her in her heart. But he had said she was the prettiest girl in the whole of the county, and that sort of made up for it. She went into the house just as the sun was going down.

The next afternoon she'd waited for Mr. Richardson for nearly three hours before she had to go out and feed the chickens. By the time evening had come around and supper was being put on the table, she'd figured out he wasn't coming for her. Her daddy hadn't said anything to her about him, but he did look at her sort of sadlike several times while they ate. The next morning she knew why.

It was all over the town that he'd been killed. His horse had thrown him and he'd broken his neck. Another farmer had found him lying in a ditch not a mile from her house. That was the cause of all the rumors starting.

She'd killed first her momma, they'd said, and now a man who'd bragged he was going to marry her. She'd taken to her room for a week, not sad that he'd been killed, but happy because he'd told people he'd planned to marry her. Her great-aunt told her it wasn't fitting for her to be so happy about the one thing the stupid boy would have regretted his entire life.

Two weeks had gone by and she'd finally left her house. She'd wanted to wear black, but again her great-aunt had put her foot down. Her daddy had said nothing, but had gone on to work in the mines. She'd been around the store three times, she remembered. No one would talk to her and she finally had to get back home. It was coming on dusk and she knew she'd be in big trouble if she didn't make it there before her daddy did.

She'd seen the woman coming toward her for a few minutes before she realized that she was a stranger. The closer she got, the more Theresa hurried along. It wasn't as if the woman was big or anything, just that Theresa didn't like the way she kept looking at her. But she was able to pass her without any words being spoken between them, and Theresa let go of the breath she'd been holding. She never heard the woman move until she was right behind her.

Theresa had waked late into the night. She was laying on a hard table and she felt...well, heavy, as she thought about it now. Getting up, she wondered for a minute as to why she was wearing her momma's good dress until she saw all the tables around her.

She'd been in the funeral parlor's back room. Getting up made her dizzy and she couldn't figure out why she felt so hungry, yet the thought of food made her ill. She stumbled to the doorway when she heard music. Following it up the long stairs from the basement, she saw the woman and a man standing next to her daddy. Before she could go to him, the woman was suddenly there.

"You'll obey me now. I'm your new master. Your father thinks you're dead and that's the way it should be." She started to lead her away from her daddy and Theresa tried to fight her off. "No, it will do you no good. I am your master."

By this time, they'd made it back to the little room where she'd awakened. She thought for sure that the woman was going to do something to her and she wasn't having any of that. Grabbing the first thing she could touch, Theresa had turned and stabbed with the long piece of a staff. The thing had gone right through the woman's head and out the back end. Theresa had been so caught up in all the blood she'd nearly been caught down there with the body. She was out the door and into the night before the first person could grab her. Theresa had been running since.

~~~

"They didn't know how the woman had managed to kill so many without being caught. If they did, neither of them said it while I was there. And the older man, Hooper, he left the area soon after. I'm checking into where he'd been from." Phil looked around the room at the people assembled there. "I really wish you would have kept this as quiet as possible."

"Peeshaw," his mother said. "You need family when you do this sort of work and we're going to stand beside you whether you like it or not." She looked around at her husband and sighed. "Is that woman Sabalz still in charge of the Trustees? Or have they maybe staked her out in the sun for us...I mean, for humanity?"

Phil glared at his mom. She hated Anye and she'd never made any kind of bones about it. When his mom smiled at him he turned to his dad, who only shrugged. It was as if he were saying, "You know how she is."

"She's still in charge. She's the one who called me in." He sat down next to Holly on the couch. "You really should try and get along with her some. She is the person who decides the laws." His mother snorted and Phil knew she'd do what she wanted, as she normally did anyway.

"So this council, the High Trustees of Vampires, you work for them?" Austin looked at Phil's dad when he didn't answer. "And what is it he does for them? I mean, besides go when they tell him to so they can scrape and bow at his feet."

Holly giggled and he turned to her when she spoke up. "It's not my fault they figured that out. All I said was the woman looked ready to have your baby when you took off your jacket."

"You told them about my title. I thought we agreed to keep that just between the two of us." They hadn't, but he thought it was implied since he didn't want to talk about it. "I was trying to keep this in perspective, not have everyone wanting to make fun of me because I'm a flipping Knight of the Vampire Guard." He knew as soon as the words slipped out he'd said more than he should have. He looked over at his father, who had paled, and his mother looked ready to burst. "That happened a long time ago. I told you she had rewarded me for my services."

"She knighted you as the Vampire Guard? Why that flipping bitch. I swear to you, the next time I see her I'm going to take her head from her shou—"

"Enough," roared Austin. Phil had heard him do that once before and the entire pack had been quiet around him for a week. "This is not what we're here to discuss. There is a murderer out on the loose and this bickering isn't going to help. Now, if the knighthood or whatever doesn't help right now, can we please table it for later?"

Phil looked at his parents, who looked both shocked and impressed at Austin. The man was a hell of an alpha to shut up his parents too. Phil shook his head before answering Austin.

"Yes and no. The why doesn't play into this, but my being a knight does. When they asked me to do this I regained several of my abilities that I'd asked to be taken from me when I stepped down. I can now track as well if not better than you and I can…."

Phil looked over at Holly. "You can now what? Tell me. What can you do that you're so terrified to tell me about?"

"Not terrified, but I am a little nervous about it. It's this." He shifted, or whatever it was that he did to become what set him apart from other vampires. "I could do this since I'd been a child. And it only got better as I grew older."

His entire body was encased in armor. Not just armor but silver armor. Normally the silver was deadly to his kind, but something about him being able to pull it over him like a cloak made him able to wear it without any ill effects. Holly stood and came toward him.

"This is what she meant when Anye told me that we were well suited." She ran her fingers down his arm and he could feel it. "She said with my abilities to track and yours to keep me safe, we were an unstoppable team."

He pulled back on the armor that surrounded his face and looked at her. Holly wasn't at all upset…she didn't even seem to mind that he could change into something that she should have feared. When she touched him again he shivered in anticipation.

Holly grinned and then stepped back from him. "What else can you do, big boy? Do you have anything else that can make you worthy of being my mate?"

"I can do all sorts of things, love. Most of which I'm pretty sure I don't want to show you in front of your family." He grinned when he heard her brother's growl. "Come here, Holly. I need to see what the armor does to you when you touch me."

He thought she'd shy away. He should have known better. She was nothing if not the bravest woman he knew. When she touched him again, this time running her entire hand down his arms then his chest, he felt her every touch. She looked at him when he said her name.

"It doesn't seem to bother me. Is it really silver or something…I don't know, something someone made to replicate silver?" Holly stepped back when her brother Connor stepped forward.

"Let me try. Maybe it's a mate thing." Before he could touch the armor, there was a glimmer then a woman was standing before them. "What the hell? Who the hell are you and how did you get past my guard?"

"I'm with him," Anye said with a frown. "And don't touch him. It will mean your certain death."

Phil noticed that she didn't touch him either and started to ask about Holly and if she would now die from touching him. Phil was suddenly afraid of losing her. He shifted and pulled her into his arms as Anye spoke to the room in general.

"She can touch him because she is his mate. Any other person, foe or friend, will die and die a horrible, slow death." Connor stepped back and put his hands behind him as Anye turned to Phil. "You should have been told that when you were given this gift."

"He wasn't given anything. This is something that he's had all his life." Phil smiled at his dad, who was quick to jump to his defense. "You'll keep a civil tongue in your head, Annie, else I'll take a switch to your hide. You know I will too."

Anye looked ready to say something but Hope, his mother, simply took a step forward. Few people knew how powerful she was and fewer still lived to tell about it. Anye took a step back and bowed before her.

"I ask your forgiveness, My Lady. I was sent here to find out what had been decided with the rogue, not to cause a problem between myself and the Campbell family." This time when she spoke Anye sounded like she was there to help and not to accuse. Phil was glad. He'd hate to have to explain to anyone why the head councilwoman was suddenly incinerated.

"See that you keep a tone befitting his title." Phil flushed at his mom's words. "What news do you have of this person? And what can we do to help get her under control?"

Anye looked confused and Phil decided to help her out. His mother, for all her toughness, didn't like to use certain words when dealing with people. "She knows that she is going to be killed. To her, that's getting her under control."

"Oh. We know that she is in the area. As is the man you told us of at the meeting." Holly snorted and it was all Phil could do not to laugh at Anye's face. "I have brought you what we have on the other killings."

Phil took the file and read it over before handing it to Austin. He looked at it a sheet at a time and handed those to Phil's father. The two of them seemed to be making some notes on what was there. But he was still confused about the holes that were in the reporting.

"It does not say who her maker is. Do we know who is responsible for this rogue? Or how long she's been turned?" He didn't like the way that Anye looked away. "What is it you're not telling us or, better yet, what you think you know?"

"The rogue was turned in the year nineteen hundred and sixteen. We know only that she was thought to be dead and when she rose, there was a…there was a problem." Anye didn't speak for several minutes and no one told her to get on with it. Phil thought everyone was afraid of what had happened. "She was taken to an undertaker. It was a poor providence so in that the girl was lucky. There was no money for her body to be preserved. And they were set to bury her."

"They didn't embalm her? How is that even legal?" Austin asked her, suddenly a fierce tone in his voice. "Are you telling me because there wasn't much money, this woman was going to be buried and would have risen anyway? Christ, please tell me that someone noted what had happened."

"She killed her maker. It was several…months before we figured it out. It wasn't until another vampire happened upon the town that he heard the story how a being was almost buried alive and that, in her anger, she burned another woman alive." She flushed a deep red before she continued. "The ash. The ash was in the room and they assumed that somehow, someone got into the morgue and set fire to a person. It wasn't discovered who the person was, nor the one who might have been the murderer."

"And the being that was nearly buried alive. That was Theresa, correct? They thought her alive and she killed the person?" She was shaking her head even before Connor had finished. "Then what?"

"They did think that Theresa was about to buried alive. She kept…she would show up on occasion and lead the people in the town to believe that since she was misdiagnosed, she held a grudge against the whole town." Anye looked around before continuing. "They think someone else, not her, had burned the person. They all seemed to think that Theresa didn't have the smarts or the ability to kill anyone. She isn't, by all accounts, very smart."

Phil didn't think she was nearly as stupid as they thought. Nor did he think that she was incapable of killing anyone. She was as cold-blooded as they came.

CHAPTER 8

Theresa caught a scent as she walked around the streets. She'd been in town for three days now and still had no knowledge of the man she'd come to find and the woman. But this scent, the scent of her first love, was close by and she followed it.

The streets weren't as busy as she'd grown used to while in New York. Night time, they were just as busy as during the day, if not busier. She'd learned to hide more during the day because anybody could come across her and disturb her sleep. She wouldn't have been able to defend herself in the almost deathlike state she'd awakened from the few times it had happened. Most of the time she slept in basements of houses that she knew where the people were gone during the day. She'd only been caught once in all the time she'd been stealing into houses.

She stood outside a house where the scent of her Gregory was the strongest. There was another scent there as well, one she'd not smelled in a very, very long time. Moving with caution she went up to the door. She nearly jumped out of her skin when she saw him on the porch sitting in a swing.

He looked older. Much older, as a matter of fact. It had been years since she'd actually seen him, and then it had been from a distance. She heard him snore softly and stepped closer to him. He had been both her tormentor and her ally for so long she no longer knew what she thought of him.

His hair was white. So white that it made his skin look papery and thin. He needed a good shave and she wondered if the men of this time used the same strap and razor her father had. She thought she'd look into that when she left there. Gregory was heavier than he'd been when she'd first seen him, and his belly hung over his pants so that there was no trace of his belt. He still wore the bow tie and she knew that it was a real one and not like the one she'd pulled off someone she'd been feeding from.

In his hand closest to her was a cup. She could smell the whiskey in it mixed with coffee. Theresa had never had coffee. Her father had never drank it, so it had never been in the house when she'd been there. She knew that if she dared a taste now it would only make her sick, so she only sniffed it for a bit and then looked down at the papers in his other hand.

She couldn't read. Not much at any rate. There had only been the one teacher when she'd been a child, and the woman had made Theresa's schooling difficult. Theresa smiled at that. As soon as she'd learned what she could do, bite people and thus kill them, she'd wasted no time in finding Miss Platte and teaching her a few lessons too. But the papers in his hand looked like something she could figure out. Before she could even get past the first word, he stirred and she leapt back into the deepest shadows.

He dumped the cup into the bushes and staggered to the door. She didn't think he was drunk, but old age made him clumsy. Going into the pretty little house behind him, she could smell the others.

A woman younger than him came from the opposite end of the house and smiled at him. Theresa had hidden behind the doorframe and held her breath. She wanted to see what this girl meant to him and was suddenly very jealous of her. She heard the woman speak only seconds before Theresa was ready to jump out and kill her.

"Hello, Grandda. I was just coming out to get you. Dinner is almost ready." She kissed his cheek and Theresa felt anger surge up. "Come on in and after dinner, we'll go over a few more things in your box."

"I got a few more notes you can add to that contraption of yours too. I've been thinking about what that man said about a few things. You think you can fix 'em up for me?" The girl laughed and Gregory and the girl faded away deeper into the house.

Theresa watched the big television while they ate. Food made her ill whether she ate it or not. There was nothing of interest on the thing, at least nothing she could figure out. There was a lot of color, which she loved, but the sound must have been broken because she couldn't hear anything.

When she heard him going into another room, she slipped into it behind him again. This room was dark with all sorts of pretty books on the shelves. While he played around with his papers and Theresa figured he waited for his granddaughter, she looked at the small toys and such on the shelves in addition to the books.

She was just admiring a shell when she heard the door open. Hiding deeper into the darkened corner, she watched as the woman sat down at the desk and opened a computer, another thing that she never got to play with.

"Okay, tell me what you have." He handed the woman a small sheet of paper like the one he'd had in his hand outside.

"Okay. Do you want me to address this to the same man or to someone else?"

"The same." He handed her something that looked like a picture and the woman got up and put it on something else. "You have no idea how much I appreciate you helping me out with this, Mary Kathleen. I would still be struggling with the first letter."

"You know I don't mind. It's sort of fun really. I know that it's been hard for you, all that mess, but for me it's an adventure without all the gore."

They worked for a while longer, and it wasn't until they were shutting down the computer that Theresa thought about getting back out of the house. When they both walked out onto the back porch, she slipped out of the front door.

She didn't know what they were talking about and that pissed her off. She wanted to go and demand that he tell her, but knew that wouldn't work either. The picture, when she'd gotten a glimpse of it after they'd gone outside, was of her. Theresa didn't even remember posing for the stupid thing. But it was her all right.

She decided that tomorrow night she was going to go to Gregory and tell him that she wanted answers. She wasn't sure what she'd get, but he'd tell her or she'd...she'd just kill that girl of his. Standing a little taller, she thought about killing the girl and having him watch. Yeah, she thought, he'd tell her whatever she wanted to know.

The next night he wasn't on the porch. She had to wait for someone inside to come to the door and that was taking too long. So she rang the doorbell and hid. When the woman came out Theresa threw the small stone into the bushes and the woman did just what she wanted her to. As soon as she walked off the porch to check the bushes, Theresa went into the house.

The house smelled strongly of the humans. There was also a cat inside, but Theresa ignored it. She looked all through the lower part of the house and didn't see Gregory, so she went up the stairs when it was clear. She was peeking into one of the rooms when Gregory came out of one behind her.

"You. What are you doing here? Get out of my granddaughter's house this minute." He shooed at her with a newspaper and she growled. "Go on. I said to get out and you'd best not be harming her either."

"You will tell me what you were doing with my picture. I saw you with it yesterday and I want to know where you got it." She moved toward him, always startled by how fast she could move. "Where did you get it, old man?"

Theresa lifted him by his neck and carried him to the room that smelled like him the most. When she put him down on the floor again, he nearly collapsed. She had to keep reminding herself how strong she was, but she didn't tell him she was sorry.

There had been enough of that, too, telling people she was sorry all the time.

"How did you do that? How did you lift me that way, you being a little girl?" Theresa snarled at him and he backed to the bed and sat down. "Didn't mean to make you upset. But you are a little bitty thing."

"Tell me about the picture. Where did you get it? How did you take it without me knowing?" Her anger surged, the horrible anger that made her feel like an animal. Theresa started pacing when she felt the room tilt. It was all she could do to turn to look to Gregory, and she could barely make him out with all the red haze. "Gregory," she said softly just before it all went black.

~~~

"It's important that you find who did this as soon as possible. I have people screaming in the streets that there's a wild animal on the loose." Holly wrote down everything her boss said to her as she glanced at the timer. Thirty-one seconds left. "And make sure you report all your findings to the local yokels. They want this solved yesterday."

She had ten seconds left when she ended the call and snapped the phone in two then took out the battery. She was tossing the pieces into the jar of nitric acid when Phil finally spoke.

"You do know that I'm going with you, right?" She nodded, relieved that he was going too. "And as for what is killing these people who do—"

"It wasn't people but a person. I think you should call that woman again. The guy's name is Gregory. I don't know why, but I think it's your girl, the rogue." She stiffened when he stood up suddenly and lifted her too. "Phil?"

"Tell me everything. Starting with why do you think it's this rogue?" She watched him stretch his neck, then he stepped back. "I'm sorry. It's just that she killed so many people and had come so close to...please tell me what you have found out."

She laid her head on his chest and closed her eyes. They had to leave soon, but she needed this very badly and suspected he did too. When he ran his hand down her back she looked up at him.

"His granddaughter found him. Her name is Mary Kathleen Matthews and Gregory has been staying there since he left New York. Do you think she followed him there?"

"Probably. Or she knew where he was all along. I'm not sure if I heard where he was staying, but she either followed him or she lives here too."

She didn't think that was right but said nothing.

"How far are they from here?"

"Less than two hours. We need to get going. They are holding the scene for me. I have to talk to the locals there and my contact said that they are expecting me. I'm going in as an expert on wild animals." She laughed at the irony of the situation. "Will you mind being my assistant?"

He shook his head before asking her something else. "How was he killed and why did they call you? Do they normally have you do run of the mill killings involving animals?"

She'd never thought of that. They hadn't and she told him so. "I don't know why me. They know that my main address is Ohio, but nothing more. I'm going to be really pissed if nothing happened and they want to bring me there to end my contract with them." She headed for the car as he locked up. "I have to go by my apartment. I have some extra guns and ammo there that I'd like to bring along."

She had more than ammo. There was the specially made bulletproof vest that she wanted to put on, as well as a few tracking devices that she wanted to hook up to Phil. She stopped in her tracks, which made him bump into her from behind.

"Can you find me?" He frowned at her question. "I mean, if I'm not close to you, can you find me if, say, something happens?"

"Are you expecting something to happen?" She nodded. "Yes. No matter where you are, I will be able to find you. You've the ability to find me too. Though I'm not sure how far reaching it is for you."

Nodding again, she got into the passenger side of his car and turned to him in the seat. "Are you attached to this thing? The reason I'm asking is that I'd like to take something with a little more...well, a lot more safety measures in it. I have a four-wheel drive baby that is plated with bulletproof glass and steel in the doors. The gas mileage sucks, but it will keep us safe if something happens."

Phil kissed her quickly on the mouth. "Can I drive it?" She laughed and told him yes. "Then let's go get the sucker. It's not a pretty pink or some girly color like that, is it?"

"No, it's bright purple with yellow racing stripes. I wanted it to blend." They were still laughing when they pulled into her parking lot ten minutes later.

"You don't spend a lot of time here, do you? Nothing here says you like it here."

She looked around the two rooms that served as a living room and dining/kitchen area. She supposed not. She'd signed the lease to this apartment over seven years ago and had probably only stayed there a total of one year...if that. There was a couch and an end table, a television set she doubted had ever been turned on, and a lamp. There were no magazines on the tables and no pictures on the walls. The kitchen had nothing on the counters, not even a coffee pot, which she would never have used anyway. The refrigerator was empty of everything, with the exception of some hot sauce, a bottle of catsup, and some packets from a Chinese restaurant, from where she couldn't remember if the food was any good. She moved to the bedroom and noticed that this room was just as sparse.

The bed had a rolled up sleeping bag and three pillows. She knew the closet held a few t-shirts and maybe a pair of pants. She went to the closet, not wanting to see how depressing the bathroom was.

The wall behind the few bits of clothing was false. She moved the clothes to the side, kneeled down onto the floor, and pulled up the carpet to reveal a floor safe. But it, like the wall, wasn't real either. She pushed down on the dial and turned it until she heard a click, then when the pad lit up she punched in the code. The entire top of the "safe" came off.

"Nice. I should see about getting one of those put into our house. Who designed it?"

She didn't look up when she answered him, waiting for the next set of numbers to be put in. "I did. It was a combination of parts I picked up here and there. I wanted someplace I could hide my guns and not have to worry about the housekeeper finding them." She keyed in the last of the numbers and the wall in front of her opened. She stood and finished answering Phil. "This wall is solid steel and was a bitch to get in here. I told the landlord it was a backboard for my bed. I was very careful not to let him help me carry it."

The door slid to a silent stop and Phil whistled beside her. "Christ. You planning the next war, or do you just like guns?"

She pulled out the Mossberg five-ninety pump action shotgun and handed it to him. "The shells are specially made with silver balls and liquid chaser. I have used this thing a few times in combat and it'll be a good gun to use on a vampire." He laid it on the floor and picked up a pair of Glocks. "Those have the same ammo design, as does everything here. I have them made for me or I make them myself."

He put both of them on the floor and reached for a double harness, which she helped him into. He put both guns in the holsters, and she pulled out a duffle bag.

"How much of this are you taking with you?" She started to open drawers and stack boxes of ammo into the bag. "Once we get this thing taken care of with the girl we can move all this to our house and set up the same sort of locking system if you want."

This time she said something. She didn't know how this whole mate thing worked just yet, but she wasn't going to be doing everything he said. She thought maybe now would be a good time to set up some ground rules. "What if I don't want to live in your house?" She put enough emphasis on the word "your" that she knew he'd understand. Apparently, he had.

He shrugged. "If you don't like that house, then there are any number that I ow...we own that we can choose from, or we can buy or build whatever you want. It matters little to me where our address is, Holly, so long as it's one we share."

She felt petty and small. "I'd like to live near my family. And the pack. Not too close, mind you, but...I'm sorry, Phil. I was just trying to assert myself and I went about it the wrong way."

"No you didn't. You're right. We have a lot of decisions to make. And the important word there is 'we.' I shouldn't have assumed anything. We can decide where we live, and we can decide what you take to the house from here." He pulled her up. "I'm sorry too. I love you, Holly, and I only want what's best for you."

She kissed him. The kiss was meant to be quick, but when he groaned she let him deepen it. The wall behind her was suddenly pressed against her back and she tried to lift her leg up to wrap herself around his hips. He pulled back from her and held her there when she tried to go after him again.

"We don't have a lot of time." He let go of her one shoulder to adjust his cock. "As much as I hate to say this, we can't do this right now. The others are waiting for us and we have to go." He took two steps back, letting her go completely. "But know this. As soon as we get to a place where we can, I'm going to fuck you until you can't walk for a week."

"Promise?"

They were both laughing when they started loading up her dark blue SUV. He told her he was happy to see that it really wasn't a bright color and was completely impressed with how much stuff she had in it for an emergency.

"I have to be ready all the time. You should see what I have at other points across this state."

CHAPTER 9

At dusk, Theresa woke. It took her several minutes to remember where she was and how she'd gotten there. Before she could move out of the dark area where she was, she noticed that she was covered in blood. Hurrying out into the moonlight, she could see that not only was it on her hands, but her clothes as well. Scared now, she looked over her entire body for cuts or something that would tell her what she'd done. She was pulling her pants down to get a look at her belly when she remembered. Gregory.

He'd made her upset and she'd turned. She really didn't know what it was called when she went nuts like she did, but that's more or less what she did—turned nuts. Sitting down on the dry pavement, she wondered if he'd been found yet and knew that he had. That girl, the one he'd kept telling her not to hurt—Mary Kathleen he'd called her—had been screaming her head off when she'd left.

She'd wanted him to suffer. When he'd not given her the answers she wanted, even though she was sure he'd been telling her the truth, she'd started biting him. First, she'd bitten his face, tore into his soft, fleshy cheek until she'd simply torn it away, and had spit it into his lap. When he continued to tell her she'd posed for the picture all those years ago, she'd bitten his left ear off, then the other. By the time he was begging her to finish him, she realized that he'd not once called out or made any other noise other than a small sound. He'd not screamed as she'd hoped, but only whimpered, something that made her incredibly more angry. And by now he lay in pieces all over his bed.

He was near death when she'd taken his throat. His blood was tainted with something…medications she supposed, because of the bottles on the bedside. But she wanted to teach him a lesson, and even though she'd forgotten what her purpose had been by then, she just wanted him to beg. And he had…not for himself, but for the girl.

When he lay dying she thought about going to find the girl, bringing her to his room, and killing her too, but there'd been no more time. She'd had to leave. Picking up the letter opener on the desk on the other side of the room, she'd plunged it into both his eyes.

"Never will you see me again, old man." Laughing, she stabbed the opener straight into his sputtering heart and watched him struggle to take his last breaths. "You are a pitiful excuse for a human being and I will enjoy killing the cop that you talked to."

A noise on the stairs made her jump back, and when the door opened, she could see the light beginning to fill the sky. Rushing by the woman in her robe and slippers, she knocked her over and was out the door before the first scream echoed through the house. Theresa laughed all the way to the house just down the street and climbed into the basement from the crawlspace just as the sun crested.

The house was surrounded by red and blue lights when she ventured back. Most of them hurt her eyes, but she stayed. She wanted to see who would come by and who would figure out that it was her. She smiled when a policeman came out of the house holding his belly. She was disappointed that he didn't puke like she'd seen them do before.

There were so many people around that she didn't need to hide this time. Theresa walked up to the house and stood by the ambulance that was opened up. She wanted to tell them it was too late for this thing, but didn't think it would be a smart move this close to the killing. She'd started for the house when she got a scent.

He was there. Phil Campbell, the vampire from the hotel, was there. She looked around, wondering what he looked like, when she saw the woman. The woman that she'd wished for days now that she'd taken out instead of the wimpy one in the back room. Moving closer to the smell, she could almost touch him when she saw him stiffen. She'd only just managed to step behind the big man beside her when the vampire turned.

Good golly, he was handsome. Much prettier than her beau Mr. Richardson, and so much taller and more muscular. She watched him as he reached out for the woman, and that's when Theresa realized that they were together. She had taken two steps forward to tear her apart when he looked right at her.

You should know that I have your scent now. And as soon as I can, I will cut your head from your shoulders and watch you incinerate. Theresa put her hands over her ears to block him out, and his laughter was still there deep inside of her head. You can't hide from me. I will hunt you down like the insignificant scum that you are.

"No," she said aloud. "No, you can't do this to me. I'm...I'm only a kid. I...what makes you think I did this anyhow?"

Speak with your mind, he commanded. You did this and more. I have a long record of your crimes against humans. The list is now noticed by the Trustees, and I've been sent to hunt you down. And so that you know, I will take great pleasure in killing you.

He moved forward and would have caught her if the woman hadn't said something to him. She looked at Theresa too, and she could see the hatred in the other woman's eyes.

What is that person, that woman, next to you about? Theresa said, speaking with her head this time. She'd never done that before and might have found it fun if the vampire she'd wanted for the past weeks hadn't threatened her with it. Well, two could play that game.

She is my mate, he growled at her. And you'd do well to keep your distance from her as well.

Theresa laughed heartily. Several people turned to stare at her, but she didn't care, this was between her and her newest enemy. She had no clue what a "mate" was, but she figured it had to be something like a girlfriend or something. She thought about biting the woman and draining her, and her fangs dropped down. Letting the two of them see them, she stepped back when he did the same. His were not only bigger than hers, but they looked sharper too.

I'm going to kill your girlfriend, then I'm going to have all kinds of sex with you before I kill you too. Brave words, she knew, but she didn't think he'd move on her with all those people around. She grabbed the first person who walked by her, pulled him to her mouth, and bit. "Fuck you," she said aloud when she dropped the bleeding man to the ground and ran.

~~~

Holly watched the paramedics work on the young policeman. He was going to make it, they said, but weren't sure what had happened. It looked like he'd been cut. She knew that he had. Phil had pulled his own knife out of his pocket and had cut across the two puncture marks before calling for help. Smart man, her mate.

"They're going to take him to the hospital now. They all believe that he fell against some glass and was lucky someone found him when they did." She grinned at him. "Well, that's what they're saying anyway."

They walked into the house, Holly showing her badge, one she'd taken from one of the many ID's that she had stashed in the vehicle. Phil had one too, but his picture identification had been stolen, he'd told the on-duty cop.

Everyone cleared out when they went into Gregory's room. Holly walked over to the man lying prostate on the bed and looked down at him. The rogue had done a great deal of damage before she'd killed him. Holly looked at the letter opener still in his chest.

"Why do they think that it's an animal killing? I've never known of any species that uses letter openers, do you? And the preciseness of the stabs to the eyes is just too perfect. I don't understand this at all." She walked to the other side of the bed and schematized each thing she saw. "There's a picture here. I think it's like the one you showed me. It's all bloodied, but still, you can see her face."

"There are some notes here too. I think he was putting together a file or something for someone, probably the other cop, Myles. These are very neatly done." She glanced over as he moved the papers into a neat stack. "I'm going to make copies and then give them back to the granddaughter. We might be able to—"

"Where is she?" a man asked as he slid into the room. "Oh my God. She killed him, didn't she?"

They both turned to the man in the doorway. She could tell that Phil was shocked. So was she. The man had gotten past five or so cops that were supposed to be keeping the room off limits to all personnel. Before she could speak, Phil did.

"It's the cop, Myles Kramer. The other man from the meeting in the hotel." He walked toward him, speaking to him softly. "Yes. Do you know who she is? Where she can be found?"

"How did you know about…have…? Did Gregory tell you his tale too?" The man looked ready to collapse, and she was glad when he sat in the room's only chair. "I didn't want to believe him. I even went up to his hotel room that night thinking I'd destroy everything in it so that no one would ever know. But I got there and started reading his notes and realized that there was just too much information there that sounded like something I'd heard before."

"So you investigated. What did you find? Other than he'd been telling the truth, what did you find out?" Holly moved away from the bed as she spoke. The man wouldn't look toward her while she stood near the body. "We know it was her here tonight. We both can smell her."

"How did you get past the police?" Phil asked before the man answered her question. "There must be fifty cops out there and you came right through them."

Anye stepped forward and Phil bowed before he could think not to. Holly simply growled low in her throat at her. When Phil looked over at Myles, he was surprised to see that the man wasn't freaking out. Phil figured most humans would be startled at someone just simply appearing, but he stared at her as if he'd seen her before.

"I let him in. He's going to need to work with the two of you, or…." She looked over at Myles then back at him. "Or he can't be allowed to remain."

Phil wanted to protest, but Holly beat him to it. "Can't remain? What the fuck…you mean he has to be turned? Into which of us? Because if I have to change him, there will be hell—"

"No, not change him." Phil nodded, understanding. Holly looked shocked, then sat down on the floor.

"You mean kill him," she said softly. "Just like that, you'll kill him as if he means nothing at all to someone."

"I'm sitting right here. And if I get a vote, I'd prefer that we listen to the young lady here. I might be a tad used up, but I don't think I'm ready to be murdered just yet." Phil noticed that he'd not even pulled his weapon, something he was sure the man had on him.

"Noted. But you must be trusted with all their secrets, as well as this man's here." Anye pointed to the body on the bed. "You've learned much too much now to be left as you are. Phil?" He looked at her when she said his name. "Do you wish to trust this human, or do we destroy a means to our end?"

"You are not killing him. I mean it, bitch. If you so much as lay one finger on him, I will hunt you down and rip your fucking ass apart." Phil stood up just as Holly began to let her beast go after threatening who was essentially his boss.

"Enough," Myles shouted. "I don't know what the fuck is going on here, but I'm reasonably sure we can settle this without killing me or doing whatever you were about to do with this…person." Everyone quieted and Phil had to hide his grin. Myles might prove to be a worthy human. "Okay. First and foremost, I want to know what the hell you are. And don't even try to bullshit me. I may be…human, but I'm not stupid. Now, someone fess up."

Phil laughed as he pointed to Holly. "She's a werewolf…she-bitch they call them in her pack. That woman there is a vampire, as am I. She is my boss of sorts, and the wolf is my mate."

They all watched Myles, who looked from one of them to the other. Then he nodded. "The woman who killed those people, she's which one of you?"

"Vampire, though she's what we would call a rogue. A vampire that has gone bad and must be—"

Myles cut Anye off. "I'm well aware of what a rogue is, ma'am. So you knew about her and are just now trying to bring her down. Not terribly smart of you to wait until she's been killing this long, is it?"

"I'll have you know we have a set of rules we are governed by. They keep all of mankind safe and out of—"

"Yeah, you've done a bang up job of that so far, haven't you? Look, lady, why don't you bring it down a couple of degrees and let these two talk? You want to make sure I know you're not at fault when clearly you are, and these two want to get to the issue." Myles turned his back to Anye and addressed him and Holly. "I got an email from Gregory last night. I was coming here to see him when I drove up and saw the circus out there."

Phil nodded, feeling at ease with the human because of his ability to adapt and frankly, to keep Anye sputtering. He glanced at Holly, who stepped to the man. Myles stood when she reached out her hand.

"I'm Holly Force and this is Phil Campbell. We've been assigned to find her and bring her down. They claim that she's unredeemable." Holly winked at him before continuing with Myles. "She might be, but that's not my decision to make."

"What did Gregory tell you in his—?"

"How did you know who I was? You said earlier that I was the man from the meeting. How did you know that? I don't remember...is it a vamp thing that I couldn't see you?" Myles grinned. "You didn't follow me up to my room later, did you?"

"Most certainly not." Phil laughed when he realized the man was poking fun at him. His respect for the cop was rising by the minute. "I was there and you didn't see me because I chose for you not to. I made you think I wasn't there. Gregory had a great deal of the story right, but not all."

"I knew she wasn't a human. I didn't know what she was, but nothing human could have not aged like she had nor torn those people up that way without someone, anyone seeing her. And she picked her victims as well. How is that? Or even better yet, why does she do this? I don't know anything at all about your...kind, but this can't be the norm." He looked at both of them before he looked to Anye. "Tell me. I have the right to know what I'm dealing with."

"Yes, and if I had the answers for you I'd give them to you. But we...she hasn't been on our books long. And her maker...she killed her maker before anything could have been done about reporting her." Anye leaned against the wall as she continued. "All we know we've pieced together from the tales from that era. The paper, if that is what they called it, had very little to say on the girl's disappearance. And the only thing that brought us to the small rural town was the death of one of our own."

"So you have a rogue vamp that you don't know, running around doing things you aren't aware of, to people you can't warn." Myles stood up and looked back at him and Holly. "Just tell me how to kill the bitch and I'll take care of this myself."

Holly snorted. "You sound like every television show I've ever seen." She made a face and raised her voice a few octaves. "Oh, help me, big, bad policeman. I think maybe a big old vampire has bitten me."

"You got a better idea? If you do then let's hear it." Holly took off her jacket and tossed it on the floor, and Myles laughed as he continued. "Oh that'll solve a lot. Getting down and—mother fuck."

Holly growled low as she stood before him as her wolf. Phil laughed so hard at the expression on the man's face that he nearly fell onto the floor. Myles tried to climb the wall as Holly got closer to him, stood up on her hind legs, and licked his face without touching him.

"Down, girl. We don't want the poor man to have a stroke." She backed away and sat on Phil's feet at his command. "Good girl. Now please shift back. In the event I never told you before you won't have to wait the hour to do so. Being my mate gives you all kinds of fun little treats. We have plenty of work to do yet."

She shifted and stared at Myles as he sat down hard on the chair again. "You're one scary bit...woman," he told her.

"No, you were right the first time, I'm a scary bitch. And so we're clear, you call me that again as a human and I'll bite your dick off and have it for lunch." She grinned. "And that's how we're going to get the bitch."

CHAPTER 10

After the coroner took the body away both she and Phil sat with Myles and Gregory's granddaughter. She was so distraught that Holly was worried about her. The poor woman had practically walked in on her grandfather being murdered and couldn't keep focused on anything around her for very long.

"He went up to bed early last night. He said that he wanted to get an early start on the files tomorrow." She stood up, handed Phil an empty cup, and sat back down. "There's nothing more refreshing than a cup of warm milk."

"You said that he'd been working hard on the files, Miss Matthews. Do you know if he kept any more information elsewhere?" Myles took her hand into his and smiled. "You're grandda was a very meticulous man. I'm sure he had some files put in a cabinet somewhere."

"His shirts had to be ironed just so. At first, I hated doing them for him, but he told me how Grandma used to iron his shirts every morning for him while he baked. He said she and him would be in the kitchen for hours just baking and ironing." She smiled at the memory. "He baked me a pie once. It was the worst thing I'd ever eaten."

Holly laughed. "My mother can bake a mean apple pie. My dad used to say she'd win ribbons for hers if she entered a contest. She didn't iron and neither did he. My mom thought if it didn't come out of the dryer neat, then you'd iron it yourself. How long had he been saving information on this case?"

"Years, I suppose. There's a large box of his stuff downstairs. He kept everything in neatly labeled files." Myles let go of Mary Kathleen's hand as she continued to tell them what she knew. "He'd set it up there first thing, his office. He told me that there were things that a woman shouldn't see." She looked at the stairs that led to the bedrooms. "I can understand that more than ever now."

"Mary Kathleen, what can you tell me about what happened? Anything." She seemed to focus on Phil for a moment when he spoke, but looked at the door again before saying anything.

"We were going to email it all to a policeman, he'd told me. Someone he'd met in one of his travels. He never said his name and if he did, I don't remember it. Do you think I should call the funeral home and make some arrangements?" She looked back at Holly. "I can't believe he's gone. That woman must have come in while I was out seeing to a noise I heard."

"She might have. I can have someone call the funeral home for you to make you an appointment if you'd like. You said there was a noise, what kind of noise?" Holly knew how to talk to distressed people. She'd had to learn how to do it in order to do her job.

"The doorbell rang. I thought it was odd because no one around here uses it. We all pretty much trust…. I went out onto the porch and then there was another noise under the bushes. I thought it was the neighbor's cat. Delilah Jane, if you can believe that. Who names their cat such a horrible name?"

"Some people shouldn't have pets, I think. I have never even owned a cat myself." Holly didn't point out that cats usually didn't get along well with her kind, but moved on to what she was working toward. "There was a picture in the room. Did you know who she was?"

Mary Kathleen nodded. "She was the one he'd had a crush on, he'd told me. She'd been…I think he told me she'd been on his first case. He said that she'd told him her name was…let me see…it'll come to me. But that was a fake name. Her real name was Theresa Elizabeth Sykes. Tessie, he called her sometimes."

"Tessie. What a lovely name. Did you ever meet her?" Phil asked quietly, but Holly was sure he already knew the answer. "She doesn't look all that old to me. He must have been very young himself."

"She died. I'm not sure if…I think he told me she'd been killed by someone she didn't know. He said he'd have to give the notes to that policeman." She looked over at Myles as if seeing him for the first time. "You. It was you. I remember now. I have your email address and it was your name attached to it. He…Grandda had me put them all in a draft and I was to send them to you all at once when he…I guess he's finished now."

She led them to the basement soon after. Holly had everything there moved to her car and was heading out of the house when Mary Kathleen stopped her. She handed her an envelope and simply turned and walked back into her house. The lock clicking home when she went inside her home was loud even with all the street noises. Holly decided to open it when she and Phil were alone.

~~~

Dallas looked over all the information in front of him. There was a great deal of it too. The man, Mr. Hooper, had kept very good notes, but the vast amount of it was a little overwhelming even for a neat person like him.

"What do you know so far?" Dallas glanced up at Phil as he walked into the room. "Shit, you look horrible. Maybe you should, I don't know, go for a midnight rum or something."

"You mean run and, no, I—"

"No, I meant what I said. A rum might do you a bit of good. Might take a little of the edge you have right now." Phil laughed as he sat across from him. "Or a run works too. But seriously, what have you figured out?"

"Not too much, but I do think that Hooper knew a little more than a human should. I believe by his notes and files that he figured she was something not human, but he wasn't sure what. There are files on vampires as well as wolves. There is also a file on mythical creatures that I've never heard of. He was very thorough, I'll give him that." Dallas handed a thick file to Phil and nodded to Myles when he entered the room and sat down. "This one is on vampires. I will be honest and tell you, while I don't know everything about your kind, this stuff seems to be pretty dead on."

While Phil read through the file, Dallas looked through another box. There were seven of them all marked with dates. Myles had told him that they were dates of the killings. But when he'd done a search, he'd found fourteen murders with the same MO. Dallas compared the ones he had information on to the list that Myles had given him. The missing seven were two before Gregory had started and the other five were dispersed between the others almost evenly.

"He didn't have any access to the Internet when he started. And from what his granddaughter told us he wasn't very savvy on a computer either. The other seven murders are on that file there. There isn't a great deal of information on those, but...damn, this guy had a lot of notes." Myles pointed to a thinner one at the corner of the table. He looked ready to say something and Phil spoke to him first.

"There is plenty of room at my house. You'll be safe there. Or there's a nice hotel in town that I'd be willing to put you up in. I know the owner really well."

"Hotel sounds good. No offense, buddy, but there's only so much paranormal a guy can take in one day." Myles left shortly after, telling them he had to make arrangements with his job. Dallas didn't say anything, but he kind of figured the guy had been fired. His mother had overheard a heated conversation earlier.

"I wonder where his source is. This is really good information." Dallas looked over at the vampire as he set the folder back down after commenting. "Some of it is crap, but he has enough notes in the margins to let you know he thought so too. Do you think he talked to the rogue?"

Dallas understood the need to disassociate yourself from someone you were about to kill. He'd only had to bring another wolf down once before, but he'd not known his name and was suddenly glad he hadn't. He figured it would haunt him more if he had something more tangible to remember.

"Yes, if his notes are correct. I think he was talking to someone, but he never mentions who. I think it had to be her, don't you think? I mean, he did have a crush on her at one point. I think there was a wolf at one point as well. He has a great deal of information here that I'm pretty sure would have gotten him killed." Dallas didn't hand this file over. That was something he'd have to talk to Austin about. "What are you going to do now?"

"I have to find her. I wish I could have taken her out at the crime scene, but there were too many people moving around and I wouldn't have been able to get her out of there without bumping into a few humans." Phil stood up. "I have to go to rest. It's nearly two in the afternoon and the sun still weakens me a little at the hottest part of the day. Will you call me if you find anything more?"

"Of course." Dallas tried not to look at the man, but he had to ask all the same. "Is Holly…is she going with you?"

Phil didn't answer right away and finally, Dallas looked up at him. "Do you have a problem with me being with your sister, Dallas?"

"No. Nothing like that," he answered quickly. "But she is my baby sister. And the thought of you…it's the sex thing, if you want to know the truth. The thought of her having sex of any kind with anyone is…fuck, Phil, she's my baby sister."

Phil laughed as he put out his hand. "You don't ask me about my sex life with her and I promise I won't ever give you reason to be concerned. Deal?"

"Deal," he said as he took his hand, but he didn't release it right away. "You hurt her in any way, shape, or form and I will tear you apart piece by tiny little piece."

"Deal."

Dallas worked for another three hours. He was exhausted and his body ached. He decided that taking a run was just what he needed. He was just coming through the kitchen when he could smell his mom in there. She was standing at the stove, her usual place, when he leaned against the jamb and watched her.

He remembered his dad sitting in the kitchen when he'd been smaller. Mom would be cooking something, as she was now, and he'd be making passes at her. As a kid he'd thought it was the grossest thing he'd ever seen. As an adult he was no less grossed out about it, but he could understand now how much they had loved each other. She looked over at him and started.

"What are you doing there sneaking up on an old woman? Are you trying to give me a heart attack? Come here and sit. I was just coming to get you to feed you. You missed lunch again." He moved to the table, but kissed her on the cheek before he sat. "You always were a flirt. For that, I'll give you an extra piece of pie."

She set a pile of sandwiches in front of him, four ham and cheese on rye, two turkey, one on rye, the other on white bread, one peanut butter and jelly with so much jelly on it that it was oozing out the sides, and crackers. There was also a pickle and three chips. He pushed the platter away, pushed her into the chair, and got her a drink of tea.

"Tell me what's wrong." When she started to no doubt deny that there was anything wrong he nodded toward the plate. "Tell me that after you take an inventory of that food. Tell me."

"She doesn't need me." After sobbing that out, she started crying. "I try my best to stay away, but I want to help her so badly. But she is so capable and organized that I feel so...so...."

At a loss, Dallas kneeled down in front of his mom. He was pretty sure she was talking about CJ and the new babies, but he couldn't be sure. Alexis was about to have her baby any day now and she was the most organized person he knew. And CJ was not. So to his way of thinking, it could have been either.

"I'm sure she needs you more than you think. I saw you with the women yesterday, you holding the baby and Alexis laughing at CJ." He wasn't sure what was going on in the living room when he'd walked in, and had beat a hasty retreat before they'd seen him. "And you cook for us all. You've no idea how much we all appreciate that. I bet they do as well."

She rubbed her hand over his forehead then smacked him hard on the head. "You are such a charmer, but you don't have a clue. Go eat what you want there and let me be. I was talking about Stacy, you idiot."

"Stacy? What does that woman have to do with this? You want to help her? Shi...darn, Mom, she's half wild, and I don't think she's capable of spending more than five minutes in this house without picking a fight with somebody."

Every time he saw her, she would snarl and bite at him like he was something she'd seen crawl out from under a rock. He rubbed his head again when she hit him a second time.

"She's a nice girl that's been treated badly. Shame on you for not seeing that. Why, that girl has a lot to offer this pack and you should be nicer to her." His mom stood up and walked back to the stove. "And she protects Alexis as if she was the world to her."

She did do that. Dallas thought she'd also make a great addition to his team if she'd stop being so— "What do you mean a great addition to this pack? Has she found her mate here?"

He didn't like the sound of that. He wasn't sure why, but the thought of her being with another male made his beast snarl. Dallas knew she wasn't his mate. He'd been around her enough to know that she didn't have a scent that drove him over the edge. Her personality did that all on its own.

"I think she's seeing that young boy, Vincent Banks. You remember him, he joined us last fall. I just wish she'd let me help her set up her house before they move in together. Here, taste this and tell me if it has enough salt."

He took the proffered bite and nodded. He didn't have a clue what it was or whether it had too much salt or none at all. He was still thinking about her moving in with someone he'd not checked out completely yet.

Going outside, he stripped down and shifted. His run was going to be hard and long, and he hoped that he'd come across just one animal that gave him lip. Dallas didn't know why, but he wanted to hurt something in the worst way. And when he was about a mile from his home he realized that he had forgotten to eat or ask where Stacy was thinking she was living.

CHAPTER 11

He was nearly awake when he felt her stir beside him. Phil reached for Holly, but she pulled away before he could get a good hold on her. He assumed she was headed for the bathroom and closed his eyes again. The next time he opened his eyes he nearly came up off the bed.

Her mouth seemed to be everywhere, his thigh, knee, calf. Before he could beg her to move upward and not down, she took his cock into her mouth.

"Mother fuck, yes," he shouted out. Wrapping his fingers into her hair, he leaned up on one elbow and looked down at her. When she grinned at him from her position he laughed. "Come up here and let me kiss you. I want to feel you slide that luscious pussy over my cock."

She released him with a small pop, but didn't move to where he'd asked her to. "I want to taste you. You just lie back and let me have my way with you. Then, if you're really good, I'll let you fuck me."

He was going to fuck her anyway. But he let go of her hair long enough to pull the pillows over and behind him. He didn't think he'd last all that long, but he did want to watch her. She went back to her task and he let himself go with it.

She nearly had him coming down her throat twice. Once when she'd swallowed him, when he touched the back of her throat. The second time was when she cupped his balls in her hand and rolled them before leaning down and taking them one at a time into her mouth and licking them. He begged her to please either finish him or move up so he could taste her too.

He moved her around so that she was now in the same position he'd been in. He didn't have any more control than he'd had when she'd sucked him, but he was certainly going to try and make her pleasure last a bit longer. Leaning down, he took her bent knees and put them over his shoulders. He could smell her arousal.

"Phil, please. I'm so close. Can't I please have a little climax right now and—" Her scream tore from her and he grinned.

"You were saying? Come again, love. Come for me so that I can drink my fill of you and play." Phil moved his mouth to her clit and licked it lavishly. "Hummm, delicious. I want more, Holly. Give me more."

Taking her pussy into his mouth, he suckled hard while he laved her clit with his tongue. The hard nubbin seemed to be begging him to bite it and he so wanted to oblige it. Pulling it into his mouth again, he pressed his finger deep into her sheath and felt her rise up off the bed. When her hands laced into his hair he closed his eyes and reached for her through their connection.

I want to drink from you here. I want to bite you in your thigh and drink while you come. Christ, love, I need to taste you.

"Please," she begged him. "Please, I want you to fuck me. I need...please, let me mark you as mine. Phil, I need to make you mine."

He raised his head and then crawled up her body. She was panting now, her hot breaths touching his skin as he made his way to her throat. He licked her pulse and then raised his head to look down at her, his body no more than an inch from hers.

"You mark me and then I mark you. I need to claim you as well. You've no…. Tell me what I need to do. Tell me whatever it is you need from me." She nodded and he watched her wolf move over her skin. She didn't shift fully, but he saw a sheen of fur ride over her before she got her wolf back under control.

"She wants you. I've never…women are the only wolves I've seen claimed. I don't…I know I have to bite you during a climax, but that's about all I know." He grinned at her blush. "You claim me and I'll…I'll speak to Mom tomor—"

"No, tonight. We'll do this tonight. When I come inside of you, you bite me with your wolf." He could feel his own beast beginning to fight for control. "When you've let her go, bite me, but make it deep. You'll have to tear into my flesh to make it true. Understand?"

Holly nodded. "And you? How do I become bonded with you? I want this for us both. I think we both need this."

"We do. I will bite you when you come. When you are finished marking me, I'll feed you my wrist. Drink from me and we'll both come again. I'll make sure of it."

"I don't think I'll need you to do much more than come in me. I'm so ready to explode right now that I can't breathe." He couldn't have agreed more. "Please hurry. I'm so close, Phil, I think I could come as soon as you enter me."

That's what he was hoping for.

He slid into her slowly. He'd hoped that would take the edge off, but all it did was make his balls tighten up around his throat. He moved slower, entering her inch by inch until he had a little more control. When she nuzzled his neck and then licked, Phil moaned. Christ, he couldn't hold on.

"Bite, love. I'm coming now, bite me." She licked him again and sank her canines deep.

His cock surged deep. He couldn't have stopped now if his very life depended on it. The harder she bit him, the harder it seemed his cock rocked into her. He had no control, none, and when she licked him again, screaming out his name again, he knew it had to happen now. Giving her his wrist, he took her throat and bit hard into her jugular. The first warm mouthful of blood slid into his mouth as she wrapped her legs around his waist and drank from his open vein. He'd never even felt her bite him.

The connection between them could be likened to a snap of a rubber band. He didn't have to reach for her to know that she'd felt it too. They were one. They were one couple as vampires and he knew that she and her pack were now one with him. Phil Campbell was well and truly mated.

He sealed the wound at her throat, knowing that he'd left a visible mark on her, and assumed she'd done the same to him. He'd heard that a truly mated couple would feel as one, but he'd never known it could be so overwhelming. He felt her every emotion, her every thought, and even her every fear.

"I will never hurt you. Never. You're mine to protect, to love, to honor. I would rather meet the sun than to harm you. I love you with all of my being."

She moved his hair from his forehead and smiled at him. "Not much of a threat considering you're a day walker."

He kissed her hand as he stared down at her. "I love you. I will for all of my days. And as my mate, that will be a very long time for the two of us."

"What does that mean for us? I mean, I know that you will live a long time, but because I have mated with you, does that mean I'm a vampire too?" She shifted on the bed and he let her. "I was wondering about children...can we have them?"

He moved to lie beside her and held himself up on his elbow. She was flustered, he could tell, but knew enough not to laugh at her. When she huffed at him, he simply looked at her breast while he answered and immediately saw the mistake in that. Her nipple puckered under his scrutiny.

"We'll live forever. Or as forever as one can who is an immortal. We can be killed, of course, but if we're very careful, we can live for as long as we want." He didn't think several lifetimes would be enough. "As for you being a vampire, I don't know. Probably not. I'm only half vamp; my father is a made vampire and my mother full-blooded. She turned him after they met and he nearly died from an accident he'd been in. They were in love anyway and it was a simple matter of her changing him when he got hurt." He took the hard peak into his mouth for a quick bite and let it go when she growled at him. "Children. Would you like some?"

"Yes, I guess. I don't think I ever thought I'd meet anyone so...can you have children?" He knew she realized what she'd said after the words were out of her mouth. "I guess that was a stupid question. Of course vampires have children. You're here, aren't you?"

"Yes. While vampires have children, they're very rare. There are nearly two hundred years between my brother and me. And there are nearly four hundred between him and my sister. I'm the baby. My parents have been together nearly a thousand years and you'd think they were newlyweds the way they act sometimes."

"I want children. I think I do. Not right now, but someday. Right now I'm too...I'm worried what my company will do whenever I tell them I want to quit." She shifted over to her side and he spooned up behind her. "I took an oath. I'm not sure what they will do to me when I leave their employment."

Phil thought she had reason to worry before, but not now. She didn't realize it just now, but she was going to be much harder to kill or to even harm than she'd ever been. He kissed her shoulder and then rested his head on her.

"I'll protect you. You just leave them to me and I'll make sure they understand that to piss you off is to piss me off, and I think I might be a bit scarier." She giggled and then settled down. He felt her body relax by degrees until she was asleep. He moved out of the bed and to the bathroom to dress. He had to go and find Myles and make sure he was all right.

~~~

Holly heard him leave. She wasn't surprised that he did. Maybe a little hurt, but not surprised. He was worried about Theresa and what she might do to the household. Well, he wasn't really worried about Theresa, she supposed, but at what she might do if they pissed her off. Holly had felt his nervousness about Myles and knew that was where he'd gone. As she started to get up and get dressed her cell phone rang. Holly knew from the tone it was her brother Austin.

"Can you come over? CJ is having a bad...she thinks she's a terrible mom because little Austin has a rash and Jane is colicky. Mom isn't here either."

"So I'm your last resort. I see how it is. Mom is gone so you call another female to come in and save your ass." She started laughing when he began sputtering. "Relax, Austin. I'll be there soon. Where is Mom anyway?"

She started pulling on clothes when he answered. "Some meeting at the library. They're having a block party in a few weeks and Mom is supposed to be in charge of the food. CJ told her to go and I thought it was okay. What do I do now, I ask you? CJ is bawling her eyes out, the babies are crying.

Connor left here an hour ago saying he was moving out. And Dallas is…what the fuck is wrong with you?" Holly laughed again. "I don't think this is the least bit funny. I'm the alpha, for Christ's sake."

"Yes, you are. And you're mean and scary too. Why, I'm sure that everyone within a mile radius of you is shaking in their boots just thinking about how bad you are." Holly laughed when he growled. "Oh grow some balls, you big baby. So what, CJ is crying. It's normal because she's is a new mom, deal with it."

Holly was going out the door to Phil's house when she remembered something else. She wondered if she was being followed and if she should be more cautious from now on about her company and the rogue. A thought to shift and run over crossed her mind, but she decided that she'd take the roundabout way there and see if she was being followed.

"I'm dealing with it. You should have more respect." She heard the baby crying get closer to the phone. "I don't know what to do with you, buddy," her brother said in the phone. "Your aunt Holly is a bitch, but I love her."

Holly got into her car and laughed all the way to the end of the drive as she made a right out. As she reached for Phil to let him know where she was going she changed her mind. No sense in pissing him off if she didn't have to. Besides, she wanted to prove to him that she was the nicer person in letting him know where she was going when she left the bed.

Be careful. I think there are others about. Theresa might have a crew or whatever she might call them. There are some notes in this list that indicates that Gregory was aware of them as well.

She smiled. A woman like Theresa would have a crew. It would make her feel like she was more than she really was, just a stupid girl without anyone to keep her in line.

I'll be careful. And watch that you're not being followed. She looked around again. They could be anywhere at any time.

He told her he hadn't driven over, but would be more careful. After telling him she loved him, she closed the connection. She could still feel him there, but it didn't feel intrusive.

She didn't see anyone at first, but by the time she had gone five blocks in her car, she knew she was being followed. Holly started to reach for Austin, but she called out to Phil through the link she'd used earlier.

I'm being followed. I don't suppose you had anything thing to do with it? She drove a full block before she turned down another street. It's a black sedan. I don't remember seeing whether or not the rogue drove a car.

I wouldn't count on it. She was only just a teen when she was turned and her family wasn't all that well off. Where are you? She could hear the concern in his voice and tried not to let it distract her from keeping under control.

I just turned onto Wilson. Do you know where that is?

Yes. I'm going there now. I have that cop with me. He and I are in the car now. I'll see what I can do about having him let me out so that I can get there quicker. Stay on Wilson so I can find you. She felt him touch her mind deeper and she let him. Holly, please tell me you're armed.

Yes, but like you, I have a lot of humans in the way that would be witnesses if I have to turn and shoot the sucker. She glanced in her mirror and saw that the car was gaining on her. I have to try and lose this guy before he gets me cornered somewhere.

Her heart felt as though it was in her throat, but she took several deep breaths. When the SUV was within a foot of her bumper, she turned into a driveway. She was glad that she'd been paying attention. One house down had kids playing in the yard. As he slammed on his brakes, she jerked the shifter into reverse and pulled back onto the street going in the opposite direction. The larger car had to turn slower as the street was lined with cars parked on both sides.

I'm still on Wilson, but I'll be on—" She nearly didn't see the other car. When it pulled into her path, all she had time to do was scream at Phil that she was crashing.

The little car was a small one that was great on gas and everything but fell apart at the slightest bump. She hit it in the hardest part, steering her own big, ugly, older car into his front, hitting the engine compartment going sixty. The car wrapped into hers and went spinning with her into the main four lanes of Main Street. She got several full windshield views of the SUV that had been coming back for her.

The last thing she saw before her head hit something very hard several more times and everything went black was the driver of the SUV that had been chasing her. Mother fuck. It was one of her own partners.

CHAPTER 12

Phil paced the waiting area trying very hard not to snarl at anyone. He'd been there since before Holly had been brought in and he wanted to see her. The short glimpse that he'd gotten of her when they'd wheeled her by him had made him sick. If someone didn't give him answers soon, he was going to—

"Where is she? My sister, where is she?" He turned to see Austin and Dallas standing at the nurses' station that he'd been barred from not ten minutes ago. He moved toward the desk, hoping the cop standing there would try and stop him. Again.

"Austin?" The big man turned to him and grabbed him. Phil wasn't much of a hugger, but he knew that as a wolf, all the Forces were. He let the guy hold him until he either got control of himself or Phil passed out from lack of air.

"Have you seen her yet?" Dallas asked when Austin let him go. "When you called, you said she wasn't here yet. I'm assuming she's here now?"

"Yes. They took her up to surgery right away. That person...." Phil pointed to the woman at the desk, who'd told him that without a wedding certificate, he was getting nothing from her. "She told me nothing. I thought about draining her, literally, but I didn't want Holly to be upset when I had to explain to her what happened."

He was trying for humor, but knew he'd failed. Dallas looked back at the woman at the desk and then at a man Phil hadn't seen before. When the guy walked to the desk, Phil figured he was going to try for information.

"Tell us what you know and I'll decide whether or not you'll get to see her. As her mate, it's your responsibility to keep her—"

"You finish that and I'll whip your bottom, Austin Jackson Force, so help me I will." Phil closed his eyes when he heard Nancy's voice. Nothing like a mom to bring a grown man back into line. "You will not threaten him like he's one of those pups. The man wasn't in the vehicle with her or she wouldn't have been as hurt as she is. Now, Phil honey, tell us what you know, please."

Austin didn't growl as Phil had heard him do before, but took a step back and glared—probably a smarter way to go on his part. Phil's own mother would have had him pinned against the wall in a heartbeat if he'd tried anything like a raised brow at her. Trying his best not to laugh at the big alpha, Phil started telling them what he knew.

"She was going to your house. She told me she was going to visit with CJ. I didn't know why because before she could explain, she asked about a black SUV following her." He didn't tell them of the terror she'd felt, nor the fact that she'd been armed. They'd not had a chance to tell them what she actually did for a living yet.

The man came at them and nodded at Phil before looking at Dallas. "She is in surgery to take care of a cut on her head. The doc said that it was to the skull and that she had a little swelling. I don't get the impression that they think there is any brain damage, but they are concerned. She has some broken ribs and a few other cuts, but I'm thinking that once she shifts, she'll recover from those. I'm taking over her care as soon as the surgeon will release her to me."

The guy walked away and Phil looked at Dallas. "One of yours, I take it?" Dallas nodded. "A doctor?"

Again, he nodded, but grinned this time. "He's not been with us long. Came to Austin just last month and pledged himself. The guy thinks that the pack here will give him all he wants in a pack and decided to stay only after a few days."

Phil nodded and then had a sudden thought. He started to say something, tell them that they should be more careful, when a nurse or whatever she was came toward them. She was dressed in scrubs and still wore the cap that held her hair. Everyone seemed to freeze, waiting for her to say something.

"Mr. Force?" Both Dallas and Austin nodded and held onto their mother. "Your sister is doing fine. I put twenty-three stitches in the right side of her head. She's very lucky. The x-rays show that she does have a concussion and a little swelling of the brain around the injury, but she'll be fine. I do want to keep her a few days to make sure there isn't anything more than that. You can never tell about head injuries."

"This is her husband, Phil Campbell. When can we go back and see her?"

Phil swore when this was over he was going to give Nancy that longevity if it was the last thing he did. She'd just saved him hours of red tape by telling the nurse he and Holly were married.

"She'll be in recovery for a few more hours. As her husband, you'll be able to go in first, but only for about ten minutes." She looked at Austin when he growled. "I'm sorry, what did you say?"

"Nothing. She's my sister and I want to see her as well."
His tone said that he was expecting her to obey him without
delay. "Now would be good, I think."

"No. I said him first. You have a problem with that, Mr.
Force, then you can simply leave my hospital." Dallas barely
caught the laugh when the doctor spoke. "Now, as I was
saying, ten minutes at a time every hour."

She went on to give more instructions, but Phil was trying
to focus on the three men that had just walked in. Two he
didn't know, but the third made him think that this had gone
from something bad to downright fucked up.

"Hello," the man said as he held out his hand. "My name
is Eli Blair. I just found out that Holly Force has been fatally
injured in an automobile accident. I've come to see what it is
that I can do for her family in this time of need."

His smile said it all as far as Phil was concerned. But
before he could tell the man to fuck off, Connor walked up and
stepped between him and Blair. Connor had moved so fast that
everyone had to step back to give him room.

"And you would be?" The question seemed to be silly
when one thought that the stranger had just introduced himself,
but Blair seemed to understand Connor's query.

"I'm Eli Blair, Holly's boss. She'd been working for me
for a while now and I knew she was in town for a few days.
Tragic accident, and I'm so sorry for your—"

"Holly's not dead." The look on Blair's face was telling.
Connor seemed to know it, too, as he continued. "Not only is
she not dead, but she'll be coming home in a few hours as
well."

Blair glanced over at the two men he'd come in with. Phil
would bet his last buck that things were not going to go well
for either of these men if this man had anything to say about it.

"I'm sorry. I'd not heard she'd been…. You must be very happy. I'd heard that her injuries were exten—"

"And where did you hear that? There's been nothing on the news yet. Hell, the accident only just occurred about an hour ago. And I know for a fact that there were no names released. I made sure of that myself." Phil watched Connor speak and walk the man backwards toward another newcomer. "In fact, I don't think anyone there was even aware that a female had been hurt much less know her name."

When Blair bumped into the second man, Phil knew that Blair knew the man. When he put his hands on Blair's shoulders and turned him toward the door, Blair didn't fight but went with him. Phil stepped to the two men that had come with Blair, reached for the one closest to him, and wrapped his hand around his throat.

"Tell me," he whispered, and reached into the man's mind. The connection was brief, but gave him more information than he'd thought he'd get. Underlings, what this man thought of himself, didn't usually have this much information and Phil had to wonder why he'd been so well informed. Letting him go with a small compulsion to call him if anything more was said about Holly or this family, the man staggered away.

He turned in time to see the doctor, the wolf that Phil hadn't gotten a name for, staring at him. Something hot, quick, and startling surged through him and he looked at Austin before he turned back to the wolf. He was gone. He'd simply disappeared.

Phil was sitting next to Holly still mulling over all he'd learned when she opened her eyes. She was staring at him when he looked up at her face and his breath caught. She looked worse awake than she had sleeping. But he leaned in and kissed her mouth gently before speaking to her.

"You're going to be all right. You have a concussion, but nothing that won't heal in a few days of rest. You have some—"

"I can read your mind, you know. I know just what happened and that you're terrified that my eye is full of blood. Please don't lie to me. We'll never trust each other if we start off lying." She closed her eyes and turned her head. "I was so afraid I was going to die."

"Holly." When she turned to look at him, he kissed her again. "So was I. You have no idea how terrified I was when I lost your connection." He took her hand in his. "You're right, you look like shit, but if you'll take a bit more of my blood, I'll be able to help you get better quicker. There are things going on here that require you to be healthy a lot sooner than you can be down."

She nodded and he felt her attack his mind. He looked around the small curtained off area as he put his wrist to his mouth and bit. As he put his bloodied wrist to her mouth, he tried to gentle her search.

"Slow down, love," he said as she raided his memories. "You're going to give yourself a headache if you continue like that."

When she suckled at his vein, he had to reach down and adjust his cock. Giving her thoughts of what he really wanted to do to her, he managed to distract her from harming them both. He filled his mind, and thus hers, on carnal images of them together in this bed and anywhere else he could think of. He was just thinking about how he could lean in and lick her pussy when she moaned.

"Phil, if you don't stop right now I'm going to scream a climax out. And I'm reasonably sure I'm in no place to do that in." He kissed her again before he told her he didn't care. "How am I?"

He licked his wrist and reached for her hand. It was hold her hand or take her right there on the gurney. When she growled at him, he leaned his forehead to hers and tried to control his inner beast.

"Broken ribs, concussion, and a multitude of bruises in places that I'm sure you will discover soon enough." He raised his head and looked at her. "I don't suppose you know who did this, do you?"

She nodded. "His name is Mervin Adams, and yes, before you ask, we worked together. He was driving, but I'm not sure who was with him. I only knew who the driver was because he kept spinning by as I was out of control." She looked away again and he saw the tears forming in her eyes. "The other man, the one in the car I hit, he died, didn't he?"

He pulled her face back to his gently. "Yes. He was dead at the scene. You're not being charged with anything because there were enough witnesses around to see that you'd been hit from behind. There are several families that came forward to say that you'd pulled into a driveway that, by all rights, should have rolled your car. And the fact that you'd picked the only driveway with no one in the yard spoke volumes for how much in control you were at the time. The other driver, the one that hit you, hit a little boy, but he'll be fine."

He didn't add thanks to him being in the emergency room when he'd been brought in, or he too would have died. A little of his blood had given the doctors enough time to save the child from certain death. But she seemed to know it anyway and thanked him.

She dozed off again and he held her until the nurse came in and told him his time was up. She was taking Holly's blood pressure as he walked out the door, and he smiled when he thought of how high it would have been had she come in earlier, or taken his for that matter. Phil ran into his parents just as he turned down the hall.

"I have the information you asked for, son," his mom said after a brief kiss to his cheek. "I don't know a lot about the girl, but I can tell you that the area she grew up in had its share of murders around that time. And they suddenly stopped, as you thought they might have, just after the funeral for this child was held."

He nodded and opened the large envelope. A picture of the girl, Theresa Elizabeth Sykes, as they knew her name was now, stared back at him. It was from a crude drawing, something that would be seen in an old newspaper clipping.

"In there is a list of the people who went missing for ten years before this girl. There's an empty casket where she was buried; they claim in the article that someone stole her body." His dad handed him another sheet of paper. "According to that, Suzanna Reeves ceased to be the day the girl came up missing. I'm assuming, like the Trustees said, that Miss Sykes killed her for whatever reason. Maybe she wasn't too thrilled about being a vampire at such a young age."

A local vampire had told the Trustees that his child, Reeves, had died several days later. He'd felt that since she was a rogue no one would miss her; he stated that he certainly wouldn't.

"She would not listen to reason. Her way of survival was to bite and then not seal the wounds. I am well and truly rid of her." He was killed three days later when the Trustees decided it was their decision to take out a bad seed and not his. And even though he'd had nothing more to do with her death than to report it, it was his attitude that pissed them off.

"And of the names on this list, are any of them still living?" He looked at his dad when he didn't answer right away. "What is it? Christ, are you saying all of them are?"

"There are over fifty names there and all but one is still around causing problems. Your girl, that Sykes child, she's their leader by all accounts. They get together at least once a month to brag about their conquests. Whenever someone has a number of kills more than your girl, she ends up killing them later." His mom looked over at his dad before she continued. "The one that is dead from that list went to the Trustees when someone in the group decided to attack someone he knew. He ended up dead three days later. That was just over two weeks ago."

He was still reading over the file when his parents left. And when his turn came to see Holly again he took it with him. She was awake now and sitting up in bed. He showed her what his parents had brought him and waited while she read it over before he asked what he'd wanted to earlier.

"The driver of the car, do you think he was set to bring you in and it got out of hand, or was he there to kill you?" He told her what the guy from earlier had said. "The guy that I touched had a very low opinion of his boss. He has only worked for him for several months but feels that he works for a goon, his words not mine."

"I don't know who he is. I've heard of some underground group that works for the same area of the government that I do, but no one has ever seen them." She lay back on the bed and said nothing for several minutes. When she spoke again, he knew she'd been putting pieces of the puzzle together. "So this guy, Blair, was there to offer up condolences because he didn't know I'd survived. Why? Because he had contact with Adams, I'm betting. Then there was the other guy with Connor." She grinned and Phil was suddenly sure she knew who he was. "Big guy with hair down his shoulders, black as night, with one blue and one silver eye?"

"Yes. Who is he? He looked like he was taking Blair out to tear him to ribbons and your brother was going to eat a big bowl of popcorn while he did it."

"Connor hates popcorn. And he does know him. He's one of Connor's snitches. His name is Randy Stout and he wouldn't hurt a flea. About a year ago, this guy came forward to tell Connor he'd been bitten by a wolf. The wolf happened to be Alexis's ex-brother-in-law Paddy. They'd been in a ring together. Randy didn't turn, which is a good thing. The guy wouldn't have survived after the first change. He's terrified of wolves."

Phil watched her to see if she was kidding, and when he realized she wasn't, he raised a brow. "Then how is he friends with a pack? I mean, your brother Connor is a big fucking wolf."

"Yes, he is, but he's more afraid of CJ. She threatened him within an inch of his life if he didn't go back to school and get an education. Apparently, she'd heard he'd dropped out of school when he'd been sixteen. When she realized he wasn't all that smart, she told him he'd either get a good job or she'd find one for him. He's been Connor's muscle since."

Phil laughed, the first real, true laugh he'd had in a long while. They were still laughing together when the nurse came in to say that her new doctor, Doctor Clint Burris, was releasing her to go home. Phil had a name now, but it still did him little good without anything to go with it. There was something about the man that made Phil think he wasn't to be trusted, and the hatred he'd gotten from the other man still made him shudder. Burris was a walking time bomb when it came to vampires, he was sure of it.

He added his name to the list that was growing for the Trustees to look into.

CHAPTER 13

She was bored. Theresa watched the humans walk around in the rain and wondered if she walked out there and killed one of them by ripping out their throat if somebody would stop to watch. Smiling, she was nearly ready to find out when she felt a presence behind her. Without turning, she spoke to the woman.

"You should know by now that you can't sneak up on me. I'm a lot smarter than you think I am. I wasn't born yesterday, you know." The woman growled, but Theresa ignored it for the most part. "What brings you to my part of the world?"

"They have your real name. I told you to not keep any part of you. Once they had that, all your information was there for them to find. That nosey bastard Phil has all he needs now to take you out. Then what happens to your merry little band of idiots?"

Theresa didn't say anything to her. What would be the point? She was supposed to be helping her, not giving out information like it was her job. Glancing behind her, she looked out at the humans again before she decided that she wouldn't have time to have fun, and turned to deal with the intruder.

"Weren't you supposed to keep them from finding me? I thought that was the deal. It's your duty to keep me safe, not help that old fool." Theresa sat on the couch and glared at the woman. "As my mother, aren't you supposed to have some sort of need to keep your baby safe? You didn't do much when I was a kid, don't you think you should be better at it now?"

Theresa hated that this woman was her mom. She'd disappeared right after Theresa had been born and everyone, including her, had thought she was dead. Theresa now wished she was, too. Her mom was also her sister, thanks to Suzanna Reeves, the woman that she'd accidentally killed that day long ago. She was the maker of them both.

"I had left your father after you were born. I didn't want to be your mother then, what the fuck makes you think I want to be now? I'm not going to help you any longer. You are on your own—" Before she could move out of the room where they'd been talking Theresa had the woman pinned to the wall.

"You'll do as I told you or else. You know as well as I do that I'm stronger and much better at this killing fun than you. You either keep them off my butt or so help me, I'll make sure everyone finds out who and what you are." She dropped the woman, stepped over her, then stopped and turned back to her. "That cushy job you have will only be there for you as long as I keep my mouth shut, Mom, so I'd be nicer to me if I was you."

Theresa was still laughing as she walked into the rain. Humans were ignorant and she loved playing with them. They also served as a way to stop thinking about the problems that Anye had just laid at her doorstep. Throwing back her head and laughing, Theresa thought about what the old vamp would think if he knew that the very person he was working for was also trying to have him killed.

Theresa didn't know why he didn't kill her at the crime scene. He'd had the opportunity. Well, he would have if he hadn't tried to save that stupid cop. She skipped along the sidewalk and thought about him and the woman. She'd found out just last night that the other woman was a wolf. Theresa giggled at that. Who would have thought there were werewolves, much less vampires?

Theresa knew she was stronger than either of the people from that night. First of all, she fed well when all they did was play at feedings. She thought about what the woman's blood would taste like and felt herself grow moist from the thought. Reaching between her legs, she lifted her skirt and slid her fingers into her slit. Leaning against the building nearest to her, she began masturbating.

People stopped to stare at her, especially men. She didn't care. In fact, she loved it. She watched as a man stopped and rubbed his hardening cock while he licked his lips.

"Show me your titties," he told her softly. He didn't come any closer, but he did reach into his pants. "Show me them. I want to see you play with them while you get yourself off."

She wanted him closer to her, but knew if she told him to that he would only come without her. She'd only had sex once before she'd been made a vampire, and after that night had figured out that the men of this time would have sex with about anything. Doing as he asked, she lifted her shirt up and began squeezing her boobs. Before long, there was a crowd of people around them, all of them doing pretty much what she and the man were.

"Come for me, little girl. Come on, come. Comeoncomeoncomeon." She hated when men or women told her what to do, but she needed the relief that only sex and killing gave her. Before he could ruin it completely for her, she came, then watched as those around her did as well. The man had his cock out and was squirting all over himself and the people next to him.

Theresa honestly didn't understand sex. It was fun for a few minutes, but after that who cared? She'd been with one person who had wanted to hold her after and pet her. Theresa had killed him for that. Grinning, she changed her thought. Okay, she'd not killed him only for that, but also for being near her when she'd been hungry; but that wasn't her fault either. Theresa had not asked to be a vampire. Even though she loved it, she hadn't asked for it.

She was moving toward the sidewalk again when she caught a scent she'd smelled before...of the older vampire, if she wasn't mistaken. Theresa looked across the street and saw the cop, the one from the hotel. Smiling, she was about to cross the street when she saw another person going toward him. Stopping by a tree about twenty yards away she listened to them talk.

"...to the other side of the market." The new guy, who smelled really pretty, looked around before continuing. "You have to stay off the streets. She will know who you are now and that's not going to go well for you. Come back to the pack house with me and we'll do everything in our power to make sure you aren't dinner for some ass with fangs."

Theresa nearly stepped to him and killed him, but didn't. Instead she saw some of her gang that had managed to work up enough money, or she supposed steal what they needed, to come with her. With a wave of her hand she motioned for them to stay where they were. All she needed for them to do now was move in for the kill before she got what she needed. They backed away and she nearly smiled. Theresa loved being a bad person. After a moment she turned back to the two men when she realized she'd missed something. Something important, she just knew it. But she couldn't think what it was.

"Okay. I'll do that. She won't know what hit her when it goes down." Then she watched as the two of them walked away and the pretty guy laughed before he continued. "Then when that happens, maybe I'll think about changing you to wolf. I think you'll make a phenomenal were."

She started to follow them when it hit her what he'd said. Changing someone to a wolf; the man was a wolf. She wondered if he knew the female, and decided that in a town this size there was probably a good chance. She turned back to follow and lost them.

"Damn it." She tilted her head and tried to scent the air when she was grabbed from behind. One of the men from the sidewalk held her.

"Come to me, little girl. I need some more of what you was giving away, and you'll give it to me." She cringed when he licked her throat. "Oh yeah, some of that pussy will feel real good right about now."

She didn't even think. Turning in his arms, she showed him her fangs. The terror on his face made her laugh as she struck him. Hot, spicy blood filled her mouth from his cheek as he screamed. When she reached behind him and felt her claws rip from her fingernails, she moved her mouth down his neck to his rapidly beating pulse. By the time she sank her fangs into his vein, she'd already ripped his heart out from his chest and held it in her hand as it continued to beat for several seconds.

Dropping his dead body at her feet, she put his heart to her mouth and bit it. The blood was still hot and she savored it. When it started to chill, she dropped it to lie on his inert body. Stepping over him, she laughed as someone noticed what had happened and started to yell, like she'd stop when a measly human told her to. Finally, she was getting a reaction from the humans. Laughing harder, Theresa walked along the street, thinking she'd need to find herself another quad of humans and kill them. She only hoped that she could manage it so the vampire and his friend the wolf was in it too.

~~~

Holly sat on the couch and watched the housekeeper fuss around the room. Glancing over at Phil's dad again, she wondered, not for the first time, how he could simply sit there and have someone wait on him hand and foot.

"You get used to it," Phil said as he sat beside her. "Dad and Mom are from a different time and this was the norm for them rather than the unusual. Besides, Sophie's family has been caring for them and our family for generations. How you feeling?"

Holly ignored his question about her health every time he asked her, or anyone asked her for that matter. As she moved to the corner of the couch, he moved down closer to her. She was going to have to murder him if she didn't get out soon. Holly needed the outdoors as much as she needed to breathe.

"Holly has been reading over the files with me. She is very good at intel. You should bring her up to speed on that woman. I think there is something off in this entire investigation." His dad stood and handed the files to him. "Besides, I think I need to find your mother. Holly here looks like she could use a good run, don't you, dear?"

Mr. Campbell left the room with a chuckle. Holly looked at Phil when he laughed. "You do know that I could have been out of this house three days ago, right? I'm going to murder you in your sleep if you don't let me out of here. Even your mother is tired of me pacing."

"That's what I'm here for, to take you to the woods and to take you on a run. There are things that I want to do to you and I want to have a lot of room to do it in." He stood up, and she did as well. "How long do you need to shift?"

She took off her robe and dropped it to the floor. She was her wolf before the robe settled. Phil growled and she moved toward the door and whined a little. She needed out more than she needed him right now.

"You have to stay close, do you understand? I have guards all over the perimeter and I don't want one of them to get startled and shoot you. They know you're here, but I didn't…you're a very big wolf, aren't you?"

She had never thought of her size before now. She knew that in comparison to her brothers, she was actually tiny. Her wolf, dark as midnight, weighed about two hundred and twenty-five pounds, about fifty more than a natural wolf. Austin outweighed her by over a hundred pounds, and Dallas only a few pounds less than that. Even though they were the same being, her wolf and her, her wolf weighed almost twice her weight. Austin had told her once that it was because the wolf in her form had more muscle mass, which weighed more than fat.

Holly sat down and looked at Phil. He was large but not fat. He was tall too, towering over her five-foot-nine by a good seven inches. His dark hair, long and straight, hung down his back in a ponytail that she had always thought of as sexy. When he moved, it was like watching a wave coming from far offshore, moving in a steady yet smooth motion until it was on top of you.

His laughter caught her off guard. "You do know that I can hear you, right? Sexy, huh? Hum, I think you're sexy too. Very much so."

Are you going to shift or watch me run? She'd never asked him if he could shift. She'd heard once that he could move in mist, but never had an occasion to find out about his abilities.

"I can shift, though I've never been a wolf. I usually stick to animals that are my size or bigger. I was a cat once." She growled at him. "Not my choice of animals either, but it was that or a snake. I prefer to walk rather than slide along my belly."

And you needed to be one of those why? His blush told her that she'd be digging deeper for that story if he didn't tell her. She laughed at him when he changed the subject.

I'm not going to run with you tonight. I want to keep an eye on you. I'll be in the sky or perched in a tree. When you've had enough, howl. I'll come back here and meet you.

She was disappointed, but not enough to not go on the run. She was excited and when he opened the door for her, she shot out into the night quickly. She was prancing in the moonlight when she felt him shifting. Looking to where he'd been she was amazed to see him shift into a beautiful bird, a large owl as a matter of fact.

Go. I don't like knowing that you're naked beneath that fur and there are any number of animals running around here that might see you. Including a few dozen humans. She took off running for the forest line and heard him laugh again. You would go to the darkest part of the back yard. It's a good thing I can smell you.

Holly ran for over an hour. Careful as she was, she only encountered one human on the property and gave him a wide berth. Watching a deer, she heard the low cry of another wolf, but knew better than to chase after it. Holly didn't want to piss off Phil, and she knew that if the male was close enough to her, Phil would more than likely kill him.

As she was starting back to the house she heard him hoot. Stopping, she dropped down and waited.

The human moved close by her. Holly didn't recognize the scent, but she knew he was someone that Phil knew. Otherwise, he would be dead if he wasn't invited. She watched the man walk past her and saw him headed toward one of the guards she'd just passed.

Holly lay low and waited, knowing that Phil would either give her the signal that she could move or he'd come to her. As she watched the two men she decided to listen in on their conversation for a little while.

"…electric running all around the property too? That's gotta run into some big bucks. How's this guy affording all this?" The guard didn't answer and suddenly, Phil spoke to her.

It's a test for the guard. He's not been in my employment for all that long and I send out someone on occasion to see what sort of information a person can get from the guards in a normal conversation. She snorted at him. Do you have a better idea on how to make sure you and everyone else on the estate is safe?

He was laughing at her, she knew, but she did actually have an answer. If the guard is a supe, then you can bet he smelled you all over your man. I did.

Holly nearly laughed out loud when Phil started cussing. He'd begun to slow down when she thought of something else. Of course he could have known you were flying about the estate, as you call it, and knew that you were watching him. Does everyone know that you're an owl?

His command for her to return to the house was funny and she told him so. She'd not listened well to orders as a child and less so as an adult, so there was no way she was going to listen to a grown man ordering her about as if she were too dumb to know better.

Would you please come back to the house? I'd like to fuck you senseless and I can't do it out of doors, as was my plan, knowing that they can smell us both.

She pretended to consider his plan, but in the end got up to do as she wanted, not what he'd told her. His low growl made her wet and she hurried along the wet leaves to get to him and let him have his wicked way with her. She was nearly there when she heard him walking toward her.

I thought I was meeting you inside. Have you changed your—? It wasn't Phil. She knew the moment he asked her what she was talking about that she'd made a mistake. There's someone out here. Someone that smells like you coming toward me. Where are you?

Above you. I don't see...wait, there he is. I don't know who it is from here. Stay there and let me see what I can find out. She didn't move from her dip in the ground. The person was getting closer if the vibrations in the ground were any indication. It's my brother. I asked him to come and talk with the guards. He also has some information for us. I'm sorry, love, I wasn't expecting him to come to the house until tomorrow.

She stood up when he told her she could and moved slowly toward the second man. Not that she didn't trust Phil's brother, but she didn't know him at all. When the man spotted her, he stopped all movement and spoke to her.

"My name is Rolland Campbell. I'm here to see my brother, Phil Campbell." He raised his hands palms out. "I don't have anything on me, just a file to give him. Do you know where he is?"

She wondered if he expected her to shift and answer him buck-naked. She growled low in her throat and he took a step back. He didn't move again until she heard Phil coming toward them.

"You can't possibly be that stupid. What the fuck, Rolland, are you trying to get yourself killed?" Phil stood beside her and put his hand on her head. "This is my mate,

Holly. And she will come inside and sit with us after you tell me what the fuck you're doing wandering around my property in the middle of the fucking night."

"Dad sent me. He has some information on your rogue and he said that it would be better if no one knew I was coming." Rolland pointed at her. "I don't suppose she'll shift now, will she? I bet she's a beauty."

He'd barely gotten the words out when she pinned him to the ground with her jaws locked around his neck. He didn't move as she bit down just enough to draw blood. Phil's laughter made her want to turn to him and see what he'd found so funny, but he told her before she had to.

"I'm thinking she doesn't care for your idea of a joke. Next time you'll remember that wolves don't share and neither do vamps." Phil turned and walked away, shouting over his shoulder. "When you two are finished getting to know each other come on in. I have a really good bottle of wine that I was going to break open when we got back inside."

She let him go and stepped back. He sat up but didn't move to hurt her. Rolland grinned at her as he sat on the cold, wet ground.

"I'm sorry. I was only kidding. I'm going to stand now and then go inside. If you'll please forgive me, I'd like to start over…once you're dressed, of course."

He stood up then and bowed before her. He was whistling as he made his way to the house and she shook her head. The man was nuts. Either that or he was just trying to throw her off her game. Running back to the house, she entered through the open door at the office and was glad to see jeans, t-shirt, and under things in a neat pile waiting for her. She'd have to thank Phil later. Maybe when his brother left. Grinning at the prospect of thanking her mate properly, Holly joined them in the living room.

CHAPTER 14

There were several stapled sheets of paper in the file his brother had handed him. He looked at them one at a time then handed it to Holly. She hadn't said a word since Rolland had handed him the file and began explaining what it was.

"Dad was doing some research on the time period. He was just telling us how when you've lived as long as he has, the years seem to have less and less meaning. Things change too quickly to get all worked up about them anymore." Phil knew that to be true. He wasn't as old as his parents, of course, but he had been a little jaded for some time.

"It says here that someone would come through the towns in that area once or twice a year and record any births and deaths for a particular area at the courthouse. According to what Dad was able to find, this kid, Sykes, was born in the early part of nineteen fourteen, not sixteen like we were told."

Phil looked at the record of birth. It was filed in the later part of the year in fifteen, but the date was what his brother had said. He was still trying to figure out why someone would purposely lie about it when Holly suddenly started cussing.

"I think she found what Dad did." Phil looked at Rolland as he laughed. "The name, look at the name of the mother."

Holly handed him the sheet of paper and got up to pace. He read down the copy of the certificate and saw the name. He looked up at his brother before looking back at the name again.

"Is this right?" Phil knew it was before Rolland said anything. "Anye Sykes is the mother of our rogue? How could she not know…or does she?"

"Oh she knows, all right. Dad said that Anye has been searching for any and all information on this province for decades. He figured she was a history buff, but he thinks now that she was trying her best to make sure all these records were destroyed too."

He looked up at his brother when he started laughing again. "What do you mean 'these records too'? Did something happen to other records?"

"The courthouse was burnt to the ground in nineteen fifteen, about four months before this was marked in the registry. The accounts were that someone left a candle burning…on every floor of the three-story building. They never figured out how the entire thing seemed to burn for hours before the fire squad was called for." He handed him another sheet of paper. "This was in one of the Bibles that Dad had unearthed a few days ago. Look at the bottom of the page."

Phil looked it as Holly sat down beside him. There at the bottom was a list of names and dates. Births and deaths had been recorded with a not so steady hand over the years until about nineteen twenty. Then one could see that the handwriting was written by someone with a younger hand and a better grasp for spelling. But he was focused on the entries for the years they were talking about.

Birted Theresa Eliseth Skyes by mouther Anye Sykes 1914~02~14

Died Anye Sykes 1914~02~16 Bleeded to deeth

Anye bled to death. He wondered if someone had found her with marks or if she'd simply disappeared as her daughter had years later. And he also wondered if Anye had sent Suzanna to change the daughter so that she could keep her with her. He didn't think either story rang true.

"What if they have the same maker? I mean the daughter and mother. What if the two of them were made vampires by the same psychopath and Theresa killed her?" Phil looked over at Holly as she continued. "Your dad said there were a lot of unexplained deaths. We've pretty much figured out that this Reeves person was responsible for most if not all of them. Who's to say that she didn't just happen upon the daughter and changed her without knowing who she was?"

"She'd know as soon as she tasted her, but I like where you're going." Phil got up to pace and think. "Okay, assuming that they have the same maker, that means if I could get a small taste of Anye, I'd find the daughter. But that would be damned near impossible, especially if she caught on. Then there is the whole—"

"You go near that broad and I'll chew your dick off and serve it up at the next pack meeting." Rolland laughed at Holly's outburst, but he covered his cock. "You think I'm kidding?"

"No. No, I don't. But I'm pretty sure we can think of more productive ways to keep me from biting her." Phil walked toward her and spoke to his brother as he did. "Rolland, go home and lock the door on your way out."

He heard his brother laugh and then the door shut. Phil continued toward Holly as she moved away from him on the couch.

"We have a lot of things to go over yet. I mean, that rogue isn't going to stop anytime soon." She moved further back. "Phil?"

"I want to see you naked. Take off your clothes and lay down on the couch for me. I need to taste you again."

She stopped trying to get away from him and stared up at him as she shook her head. "It's my turn. I want to see you naked and suck your cock until you come. I haven't had a lot of opportunity to do that to you." He moved closer to her when she reached for him. "Come here, Phil, let me have my way with you."

He pulled his shirt up over his head and tossed it on the floor. Holly ran her finger down the zipper of his pants before she moved to his belt. As she unbuckled it, he thought about her mouth taking him and his cock ached to feel her.

"I've thought about this all night," he told her. "But my plan was to take you outside. I was going to press you against the nearest tree and fuck you." She pulled his belt free of the loops and then kissed his navel. "Christ, love that feels good."

She twirled her tongue in his crevice then rubbed her cheek over his covered cock. He laced his fingers into her hair as she unbuttoned his pants. She moved the zipper down the teeth one at a time and he was ready to snarl at her to hurry when she finally reached into his pants opening and fisted his cock. Even before she had him free of his opening, she had her mouth over his engorged head.

"Humm," she hummed, and he threw back his head. He looked back down at her when she shifted off the couch and onto her knees in front of him. "I want to feel you fuck my mouth. I know I have to swallow you to have you fit, but all I can think of is having you fuck me this way."

He couldn't answer her. He nodded, about the best he could do with her where she was. As she moved his pant legs down and off him he watched her lick him, suck him, and fondle his balls.

"Roll them in your mouth," he told her in a strangled voice. "Take my balls in your mouth and suck them too." She did as he asked and he moved as gently as he could against her cheek with his cock. He wanted to ram it deep in her throat, but was afraid of hurting her. He was thicker than most men and well endowed. He guided her head back to his cock when he'd had about all he could take of his balls being in her mouth.

She caught on quickly. Before he could teach her how to take him deep in her throat, she was wrapping her hands around his ass and helping him fuck her. With his hand in her hair, he moved it so that he could see each time his cock moved in and out of her. Her eyes were closed, but he could feel her excitement, smell her arousal and, Christ, he could almost come like this with just her mouth on him. Lifting her by her hair, she let his cock go and he growled when she tried to take him again.

"Strip. Then over the couch. Lean over the back of the couch and hang on. I'm going to fuck you. Hard, fast, and quick." He wasn't kidding. He knew that as soon as he entered her he was going to come. He only hoped she was as ready as he was or she was going to be slightly disappointed.

She stripped out of her clothes so quickly that he was a little saddened. But as soon as she was naked, standing before him, he was glad for her years of practice of stripping down to shift.

She stood behind the couch and he moved up behind her. When she opened her legs wide he could see her juices as they streamed down her thighs. He wanted to lick her clean, but knew that if he did, he'd have to bite her and he wanted to feel her pussy tighten around him as she came. Fisting his cock, he moved the head in her juices as he leaned over her.

"You are wet enough that I could fuck you for hours and you'd not be sore." She moaned and he nipped at her shoulder. "My cock is so full that I can't wait to feel it come inside of you deep."

"Please, Phil. I need to feel you inside of me." She moved her ass back to his cock and tried to reach for him between her legs. Her hot fingers grazed his tiny eye and he felt his balls tighten up to his body.

Guiding his cock to her entrance he moved in and out of her to just his head. She moaned again and he wrapped his hands around her hips. He saw her grab the back of the couch and hang on. Phil couldn't wait any longer. He slammed into her deep.

"Mother fuck," he shouted as he pistoned into her. She met him stroke for stroke as he took her, and as soon as he felt his cum rush to fill her, he leaned down and bit her shoulder deep. Her climax screamed from her. He reached around to her clit and pinched as he suckled hard, bringing her to another powerful climax.

Again, he told her through their link. Come again for me. As she came for the third then the fourth time, Phil fed from her. Her rich, thick blood filled him in ways nothing ever had before. When he'd had enough he licked her wounds closed and then bit his wrist to give to her. As soon as she wrapped her mouth over his vein he felt her come again. He, too, even as spent as he was, came again, his body exploding inside of her as she milked him dry.

When Holly collapsed over the couch back, he pulled his wrist away and sealed the wound. He leaned over her without strength for several minutes, wondering how on earth he'd lived this long without her. When he thought he could carry her without dropping her, he lifted her in his arms and carried her to their bedroom.

He watched her sleep after he lay her down and crawled in beside her. She was curled to her side with her right hand under her cheek. He moved her hair from her forehead and she sighed gently. Phil was in love with this woman, had been for nearly five years. She moved closer to him and spooned into his body. Wrapping his arm around her waist, Phil closed his own eyes.

He wanted to catch this rogue and then he was going to make it his life's work to make sure Holly was happy. He decided that he was going to take her away for a while. Somewhere she could run when she wanted and they could make love anywhere they felt like it. He made a mental note to talk to her about her job. She needed to let her family know what she'd been doing.

He had a moment's thought about the man, the one who'd tried to kill her that day, and yawned. Smiling, he realized she'd worn him out. Tomorrow they would talk. Tomorrow, they'd have a family meeting and they'd get everything out in the open.

~~~

The meeting the next morning wasn't going well. Holly looked over at Phil and decided that she was going to smack him. He was grinning like a loon and she knew it was because Austin and Gordon were pissed off. She put two fingers in her mouth and whistled. Everything came to a halt.

"Now that I have your attention, I would like to finish." CJ giggled and Austin glared, but they didn't speak. "I have been working undercover for nearly nine years. I'm very good at what I do. So good, in fact, that I have been promoted eight—"

"You're a hired killer," Austin exploded again. "You kill people for money and you expect me to think just because you're good at it that I'll just—"

"So help me, if you say anything that even sounds like I need your permission to do it, I will show you just how good at my job I really am." Austin's mouth shut with a snap and Holly continued. "As I was saying. I'm very good at my job. Not just the killing part, but the tracking, the way I get to the heart of the matter before I finish up. I've been on several jobs where all I did was track. And no, before you ask, no one knows what I am."

At least she didn't think they did. The text she'd received that morning had her thinking that someone on the inside knew she was wolf. She ran her fingers over her pocket where the phone rested and wondered if she should have told Phil, then dismissed the thought. He had enough going on right now without her adding to it. She looked over at Dallas when he spoke.

"Who is it you work for actually? I'm assuming that it's something in the government. Any initials that will make me know something more?" She grinned at his wink. "You know you can tell me. I'm gonna find out soon enough anyway."

"No. And you won't search either. Not yet at any rate. Leave it be for now." She sat down on the arm of the chair Phil was sitting in. "But I do need your help. Not really so much your help as I need you to keep an eye out. I think maybe I might be being followed." She waited for the shouts and wasn't disappointed. She let them go on for a few more minutes then simply put her fingers in her mouth to whistle again, when Phil stopped her with a hand on her thigh.

"They need this. One thing I've learned over the years with this group is that they do better with arguing. I believe it's their way of dealing." They both watched them and when they calmed a bit, Phil continued. "The person who is looking for her drives a dark SUV. He's the one that hit her a few days ago. I have a bit of information on him and the best part is that he's been dead for several years. Same as your sister."

Holly was surprised by that. She knew that she was declared dead in the company, but she also used an alias, even within the company. No one knew her real name, and she had made sure they didn't know her family either. That was what had scared her so much about the text.

Tell me what it said, Phil whispered. I thought you'd tell me before now, but if you're this scared, I can no longer wait for you to get around to it.

It's nothing really. She felt his small surge of anger, then his love. She felt bathed in it. It said that I wasn't as safe as I thought.

What did it say exactly?

She didn't answer him right away, just realizing that he was speaking to her through their link and her family too.

I've had a great deal of practice handling two conversations at once. Stop procrastinating. Tell me.

Holly Force, I'm going to enjoy killing you and that bat you are fucking. She shifted on the arm of the chair before she continued. I don't go by Holly Force in the company. I'm Heather Wells.

"There's been a few changes in what Holly has told you," Phil blurted out. "She's not just being tagged, but someone wants her dead."

"What the fuck?" Holly said to him as she jumped to her feet and stepped back out of his reach. "What the hell are you doing? I told you that because I thought you'd keep it between us."

The room around them erupted just as she thought it would. She ignored it as she and Phil argued. The moron had just put her family into danger, and she was going to show him how pissed she was. Before she could think about what she was doing, she shifted and lunged at him.

CHAPTER 15

Theresa let the room's voices flow around her. She fed off the energy from the shouts and heated arguments. She thrived off their stupidity, and also their ignorance of what they were.

They all knew they were vampires. It would have been impossible to have hid that from them, but there were other things, things that she'd only just figured out on her own. Like feeding off the emotions of those around her. She couldn't live off it, but she could get a quick fix. She shifted in the chair that she had claimed for her own and waited for the high to slow as the voices calmed a little. She opened her eyes when she took a deep breath.

"Are you all with me now or do I have to kill someone else for you to realize who's in charge?" She glanced over at the pile of ash that she left there every time she killed one of them, all two of them. It wasn't as many as it looked, of course. She'd brought in some soot from a fireplace and put more and more on it daily to make herself look all "bad assed." She grinned at the term she'd heard a few days ago.

"I don't understand how you can be so calm when the big guys are looking for us." She simply smiled at Peter, the newest vampire to the group. "What are we being targeted for anyway? For feeding?"

Technically, the Trustees were only looking for her. But she thought that if she told her posse, another term she'd learned recently, that she was the one they wanted, they might turn her in for the reward. She stood up and he bent at the waist before her.

"They seem to think that we're not supposed to feed from people but each other. They want us to drink each other's blood and then die." She'd seen what happened when a vampire drank from another, and she shivered with the memory. "I think they want to be the only vampires in existence and want all of us underlings to die."

Anye had come to her last night and told her that Holly Force and Phil Campbell were looking for her and were going to kill her as soon as they found her. Anye said she didn't know why other than they had some sort of grudge against her. Theresa didn't believe her, but she was thrilled about having their names confirmed. She'd known who they were from the hotel, but she'd not asked them if those were the names they went by. She was also surprised to find out that Holly was some sort of killer. She'd not thought that by looking at her, and Theresa thought her mother was lying to her to scare her. Anye told her that werewolf blood was by far the best to live off of. Theresa couldn't wait to find out. She licked her lips when she felt her fangs drop.

"Then we're all doomed." One of the others, someone Theresa couldn't put a name to if her life depended on it, nor did she care to, flopped down on the filthy couch. "We might as well go on in the sun and end it for us."

Theresa was at her throat in a heartbeat. She wasn't startled by how fast she could move this time, but was thrilled for the way it happened. The girl was just about to die, only she didn't know it yet. Lifting the girl up, she held her high then tossed her away before she turned to the rest of them.

"We will end them before they do us. Do I make myself clear?" They nodded to her and she knew that they wouldn't talk like that again. "As of right now, we're gonna find that bitch and make her pay. But the vampire? He's all mine."

And he would be too. Theresa had decided that he was going to fuck her. She knew he'd be good at it too. Nothing like the stupid babies she'd been with, but a real man. She moved to the chair again as her people dispersed.

Her people. She'd been running this group for nearly a decade and she was tired of them. Thinking about how she was going to get rid of this group, she felt the air stir around her. The second her "mother" walked into the room Theresa was ready for her.

"Who did you tell?" The first slash of the blade hit Theresa across her cheek. It burned like fire and she jumped back as she lunged at her again. "Who did you tell you were my daughter?"

This time Theresa was able to hit back, not as hard as she'd have liked, but hard enough to knock Anye to the floor. She stepped back quickly before she answered. "I don't know what you're talking about. Do you honestly think I want people to know who you are to me? What the heck is wrong with you?"

The wound at her cheek continued to bleed and Theresa licked her thumb and ran it over the open cut. It still bled, but didn't hurt nearly as bad. She bit her palm open and rubbed her blood over the cut and could feel it begin to seal. She wondered briefly why it hadn't healed on its own.

"They know. I don't know how they found out unless you told them, but they fucking know. The Trustees are asking me all sorts of questions as if I had something to do with what you are." Theresa had a second to be hurt by the comment, but Anye wasn't finished yet. "They are asking me to give my blood to the knight. Telling me it would go faster for me if I cooperated."

Theresa didn't understand why they wanted her to spill her blood to the darkness. Night wasn't really anything to be afraid of, and she was about to say so when Anye ran at her again. She was quick, almost quicker than Theresa remembered her being, and she was barely able to get out of the way before the blade sank into the chair she'd been standing next to.

With a roar she attacked. Theresa ran at Anye with a pipe she'd hidden a few days ago when she'd been playing with a human. It still smelled of blood and fear, and she nearly missed her mark thinking about when she'd licked the pipe clean. She'd had so much fun that night. This time she was able to hit her.

The pipe broke her jaw and her cheekbone, if Theresa didn't miss her guess. There was a crunching sound and, for a few seconds, a wheezing that sounded like Anye was having trouble breathing. Theresa didn't go to see, didn't even get close enough to smell. She watched the wounded vampire as if she knew she was going to attack no matter how much pain she may or may not have been in.

"You fucking whore," she shouted at her. "You mother fucking whore. How dare you hit me? I'm the counselor of the Trustees, the highest ranking officer in the whole of vampires."

Theresa took several steps back from Anye, knowing somehow that this woman was beyond just mad, even beyond pissed. She was in a murderous rage. When she picked up another pipe and held it in front of her Anye laughed.

"You moron. You really think you can hurt me? What do you know about power and age? I may be a mere few decades older than you, but I have been taught while you stumbled around like a babe at her mother's tit."

Theresa was suddenly afraid. She hadn't been taught. The first time she'd stumbled over her meal of the night, she'd been so afraid she'd not fed for over a week. And then when she had again, she'd killed three people trying to figure out what had happened to her.

"My mother's tit, as you well know, wasn't there for me. You didn't even hang around long enough for me to be named. Father said you'd died giving birth. But I guess the night called to you." Theresa attacked again. One pipe missed its mark while the other broke Anye's arm. "I will break you apart one piece at a time and spit on your ashes afterward."

When Anye rushed her this time, Theresa fell backward. She knew she was going to die as soon as Anye fell atop her. The claws that morphed at the end of her hand both terrified and fascinated her. So much so that when they came toward her throat Theresa felt excitement rush through her blood. But at the last second she moved and knocked Anye back. The older vampire moved then, faster than Theresa had ever been able to. First she was standing in front of her, then she was at her throat. Theresa tried to get loose, but all she managed to do was tear her fingers from her hand, sending her mom screaming into the night.

~~~

His phone going off woke him. Phil wasn't sure who it was; the ringer was the default one, but he knew for someone to call him this late in the afternoon, it had to be important. He answered it cautiously.

"Anye Sabalz just came to me with her hand nearly ripped from her body. She claims that she doesn't remember what happened. You should also know that we've got a location as to where the rogue and the others have been hiding. Won't do us much good now, mind you, because the house is burning as we speak." Phil heard Myles laugh and was worried for the man as he continued. "They are trying to get it under control, but the entire area is going up."

"What else has happened, Myles?" The man laughed again and Phil looked over at Holly as she rose from the bed to go to the bathroom. "Tell me."

It was hard to compel someone to tell you what you wanted over the phone, but apparently, it worked. Myles started crying the moment he started talking. For a grown man to break down like this had Phil beyond worried.

"She killed four others. Humans, I guess you call them. They were camping out in the upper floors. Or so the police here are saying. I saw one of them. They had been…she'd been…I guess she'd been using them." Phil closed his eyes, knowing there was more and dreading it. "They were babies. One couldn't have been much more'n ten or so. The youngest was a kid. I'd say six or seven. They couldn't have gotten out if they'd been able to move. She had them near death when…the coroner said that they'd been drained or something. I'm thinking she had them chained up to one of them old fashioned radiators. They were alive when they burned up like they did."

Phil looked over at Holly when she came out dressed. Her entire outfit was black from the top of her head to the shoes on her feet. He nodded. They were going hunting and there was no reason to hide it.

"Tell me where you are." Myles gave him the address. "Holly and I are on our way. We should be there in about ten minutes, less if I can convince her to let me take her." She nodded when he looked at her. "Don't say anything to anyone that you called us. We'll be there shortly."

Holly was wrapping her body around his when she asked something he'd only just thought of. "How did he know that the rogue was there? I mean, I know enough about vampires to know that their sense of smell is extraordinary, but he knew she was there. How?"

He knew she'd missed part of the conversation and he related the part of Anye going to Myles. "I didn't think to ask him why she'd go to him and not to someone she knew she could trust. Could she be trying to cover her ass? I would be." Phil kissed her mouth then grinned at her. "Hang on. I'm going to move us very quickly and I don't want to drop you on the way."

"You do and you'll be very sorry." She buried her face in his neck and her hot breath made his cock thicken where she wrapped around him the most intimately. She looked up at him. "Seriously? We've done nothing but fuck since I moved in with you."

"Yes we have, and you've enjoyed every minute of it." He swatted her hard across her ass. "Now behave or we'll be late and you'll have to explain to Myles why I had to stop long enough to fuck you against the wall before we left."

Christ, his entire body hardened when she groaned. He was going to have to move her off his cock now or really fuck her. Her soft folds were very tempting spread over his cock the way she draped over him. Wrapping both his hands around her ass, he did press her against the wall before he moved to a safe place to move. She growled this time and he could smell her. They were going to kill each other at this rate.

The crime scene tape was everywhere. It didn't stop him or Holly, but it did slow them down. They found Myles at the far corner with a group of uniformed police officers. None of them looked happy to be there.

"Anye is spilling her guts to that other guy. I don't know who he is, but he keeps hissing at her and showing her his fangs. Tell me," Myles asked suddenly, "do your fangs get bigger the older you get?"

Phil didn't answer. He didn't figure Myles was serious and he wasn't sure the man could handle the information. Yes, fangs did get longer as a vampire aged, and sharper as well. He wondered what the human would think if he knew that as a vampire, Phil could find every person he'd ever bitten and tell just where he'd fed from them. It would probably freak him out. He knew that there were times when he was a little overwhelmed by his knowledge too.

The man that Anye was currently speaking to was her second. Jose Benson was older than Anye and a great deal less tolerant of today's actions. Phil walked up to him and bowed low. Jose growled low before he spoke.

"You're a good deal older than me and a great deal more experienced. Had you taken this job when it was offered, this mess…." He looked around the area before continuing. "It would now be your problem and not mine. Do not bow before me, knight. I have enough going on right now to be worried that you might break a hip."

Jose's laughter was chilling and made the hair on his neck rise. Phil looked over at Holly when she came to them, and laughed again when she too bowed before Jose and earned another growl.

"What is to become of her? She's not as innocent as she has led us all to believe. We've found…evidence that she not only knew of the rogue, but is related to her by blood as well as being her sister from the same maker." Holly growled at Anye when she tried to deny what she'd just said. "I don't lie, vamp, and you have made a living from it. Behave or I'll snap your neck like a chicken."

Jose glanced down at Anye before he spoke. "She is going to be staked when this is over. For now, she is going to give you her blood so that you may find the rogue. She will cooperate or she will not. Either way, you are to taste her."

Phil didn't say what was really on his mind about staking the former Trustee, but thought the man knew what he was thinking. Anye had been the center of this since before she'd been made what she was. She should have been killed long ago. But he looked at Holly before he answered about the blood. Holly had been quite clear on what she would do to him if he even tried to bite the Trustee.

"What will happen to my mate if he takes her blood and she is killed?"

He didn't answer her, letting Jose do the talking. He thought he might be safer if he didn't.

"He will do as he's told. I am the one who is in charge now and I will—"

Holly could move fast, that was true, but Austin was just a tad quicker it seemed. Until that moment, he'd not even known the man was there but apparently someone had given him and the entire Force pack a call to arms.

Austin had the man by the throat and up in the air before Jose had a chance to finish. Austin let a little of his wolf go and stood holding him with fur covering his body and his claws digging into his flesh. Phil was sure that given a reason, even a small one, Austin would break Jose's neck and simply walk away.

"You'll keep a civil tongue in your mouth or I will take it from you. Then I will feast on it as you watch. This is my sister, you bloodsucking asshole, and I protect what is mine. Her mate there"—he nodded to Phil as he continued—"will do what he wants, not what you think he should. Do I make myself perfectly clear?" Jose nodded. "Good answer.

Disappointing, but a good answer. I'm going to let you down now. And so you know, I intervened on this not because Phil can't protect his mate, but because I figured you'd live to your next breath if I took you instead of him doing it."

Jose dropped to the ground and incredibly, he started to attack Austin. Dallas and Connor were there before he could raise his clawed hand. Phil spoke before things got too much more out of control.

"Think, Jose. Think very hard. There are nearly forty wolves here and all of them loyal to that man. You strike and you are as good as dead." Jose looked at him, his eyes red as his anger boiled through. "Is your being angry at this situation worth dying for?"

"He should learn his place. He isn't to…." Jose seemed to gather himself as he stood there. He looked back at Anye then at him. "Finish with her. I need to kill someone and it might as well be her."

Phil nodded then grinned. "Thank you, my friend. Austin would have made a mess of things and, right now, I simply want to go home and fuck my mate. But as for Anye, I cannot take from her what is not freely given. It is the code of the knights. And as I am mated, she will need to take from her as well."

That wasn't entirely true and Phil was pretty sure that Jose knew it. Technically, as a mated knight, he should have been removed from service. But as he'd made the rules, he didn't have a problem with bending them to suit himself. Besides, he was pretty sure that Holly could help him if she could rely on her own senses rather than his.

"So be it." Jose stood near them as they both took from her offered wrist. When they had both stepped back Jose picked up Anye and tossed her over his shoulder, then looked over the people gathered around them. "Kill the rogue. I want her dead before the next rising. And if you need to have more involvement of your new family then you will do well to tell them that they will answer to me if there is ever a word about this to anyone."

"They will keep us safe." Phil didn't even look at Austin when he growled. He knew as surely as he was standing there that Austin would die before he gave him up. CJ would kill him. "I swear to you on my oath."

Jose nodded once and disappeared. Phil thought he heard Anye screaming as they misted out of sight.

CHAPTER 16

Holly had her scent. Not only that, but the blood she'd taken from the woman had made her feel euphoric, energized, and like she could take on the world. She slowed in her movements as she felt Phil near her. He entered her mind and she lay down to listen.

Would you mind, oh, I don't know, waiting for me? He sounded pissed and his next words confirmed it. Holly, so help me, when I catch up with you, I'm going to wring your pretty neck.

She hadn't thought. I'm so sorry. You have no idea how…do you feel it? She didn't know what she was feeling really, just powerful along with everything else. Her blood is like a major hit to my system. I couldn't wait there any longer.

It will wear down. But for now I need you to wait. I'm coming to you, but so are your brothers. And just so you know, Austin is not a very happy wolf either.

She could feel his anger as he got closer…or she thought it was him. But at the last second she could only watch as something, something incredibly fast, snatched him out of the air just before he reached her.

Austin! she screamed in her head as he disappeared. She moved toward where he'd gone only to come up against a large wall in the form of Phil.

Don't move, he whispered through her mind. It's not only the rogue, but beings who smell like her with her. I think it's—

People appeared. There were six of them, all vampires, and most of them as young as a year or two old...not their actual ages, but how long they'd been vamps. She didn't know how she knew that and looked to Phil for answers.

It's what I can do. If given enough time, I can give them the exact date and time of their conversion. But these people, these vamps....

When he didn't finish, she did for him. They're starved. All of them but her.

And she wasn't either. She stood proudly among the men and women around her and looked ridiculous. It was then that Holly saw why she stood out. She wasn't just healthier than the others, but well dressed and clean.

"Where have you taken the alpha? I demand that you bring him to this field now." Phil's voice rang over the field loudly. "As a master over you, I demand your compliance."

Holly saw her shift on her feet. The young girl fought against the command and nearly gave in. She saw the moment that she was able to throw him off. But she knew it wouldn't last. Holly knew this as well.

"You aren't my boss. I'm my own lord and master. I'm powerful and you, you're nothing more than an old fart that can't possibly see me for what I am."

Holly raised a brow at the girl and Phil laughed. He laughed so long and so hard that he had to grab the tree next to him to stand. Just before Holly thought she'd have to have him committed, he flashed to Theresa and held her up by her throat high off the ground. When the others moved as if to go after him, he raised his hand and they all dropped to the ground.

"You've no idea what power is, little child." He shook her once and Holly heard her teeth rattle. "You've managed to hide for a long while, but now I have you. You'll stand before a council and you'll be tried. Or…."

Theresa didn't fight against the hold, but did put her hands on Phil's. She looked…well, Holly thought she looked too relaxed, too sure of herself. When she grinned down at Phil, she finally asked him, "Or what?"

"Or I get to kill you. Tear your head from your shoulders while your black heart still beats. It would be my pleasure to kill you, as a matter of fact. So please," he said as he shook her hard enough that Holly heard her teeth bang together. "Please make it so that I have to kill you."

It happened quickly. One moment Holly was watching Phil hold the rogue, and the next, he and the girl were gone. Before she could see where they'd gone her brother came limping across the field, his wolf covered in mud and blood. She was at his side in seconds.

"What happened? Where did you…? Are you hurt?" She couldn't find a place on him where the blood had come from, so she threw him to the earth and checked his legs both front and behind.

His low growl made her look at his face. His eyes were filled with pain, but when she started to check him again, he growled.

"All right, then where? I can't find a frigging thing wrong with you." She rubbed her hands over his muzzle and he whimpered.

"It's his…you might want to check his mouth. I think that's where he…where he might be hurt." One of the vamps that had fallen when Phil took the girl sat up. He made no move to come to her and she was glad. He didn't look much older than seventeen.

Holly opened her brother's mouth and saw that he'd lost a tooth. Not one in the front, but a molar in the back. Plus, it looked as if he might have bitten his tongue. She looked over at the boy again.

"How did you know?"

She watched as he looked away, then he answered her. "I was a vet. Well, a vet's assistant. She...the kid, she took me one night when I was coming out of work and bit me. Said I'd have a better life and she was lonely." He laughed without humor. "Some life. I can't do what I've always dreamed of because some bloodsucking bitch decided she was lonely and thought that changing me to the monster she is would be a lark."

She could feel his anger, but she could also feel his need to come to Austin's aid. She moved back from her brother after taking a deep breath, and asked the kid to see where else he was hurt. Austin looked into her eyes, but he didn't growl when she moved further back from him and the young man.

"He needs fluids. I'm guessing...I never knew there were wolves that could change. Hell," he laughed, "I didn't know there were vampires either until now. Can he...shift, I guess it's called?"

"Soon." Austin would have to wait at least another twenty minutes before he could. She didn't tell the man that, but watched as he gently looked him over. Even when he found a bloody wound on his left shoulder, Austin lay very still and didn't snarl at him at all.

"I'm Alexander Hawkings, by the way. You're Holly Force. I met you a few years ago when your family...Dallas, is he your brother?" She nodded at his question. "He interviewed me for a position as doctor. I didn't understand why they needed a vet back then." He laughed again. This time, she could hear the humor. "I guess he was getting someone to care for his people."

"Yes. But the man you're helping, he's the alpha, the big cheese, I guess. Austin Force is my brother, as are Connor and Gordon." When he moved back, she could see that Austin was sleeping. "You put him to sleep?"

"No!" he shouted then seemed to gather himself. "I mean no, not to sleep. I can put people in a sort of restful state, but I'd never...." He laughed again and then looked at her. "You simply meant asleep. I'm sorry. Where I work...worked, putting someone to sleep had very little to do with a restful state."

She grinned too. She heard him before she saw him and stood up. Phil was walking toward her and he was alone. She stood up and noticed that other than Alexander, everyone else was still out.

"I've taken her in. She has been put behind silver bars and will remain there." Phil glanced over at the young boy then back at her. "He's been near you."

"Yes. But not touching." She knew that vampires were very territorial. She also knew that he'd kill Alexander if he so much as moved right now. "He is a vet and has helped me with Austin."

Ignoring him for the moment Phil continued to talk about Theresa. "The Trustees took her. The trial will be set for the week after next. I told them that you and I would be there. Is that all right with you?"

"I can help." They both turned to the girl who spoke, and to Alexander. "We all can. None of us were...I'm not sure what it's called, but none of us were made what we are because we wanted to be."

"Converted. And how many of you are there? Surely there are others, older than you?" Phil nodded to the others. "None of you are much older than a year. The rogue, she's been around for nearly seventy years. Where are the others?"

Alexander cleared his throat. "We're it. Last month, or the month before, there was this woman, but...." He looked at the girl. "Shelly, when was the last time you saw Anye?"

"Could be a couple of weeks. Don't know. She hates our boss. Man, you should see the two of them go at it. Like they wanna kill each other but can't. Anye said there was a law about killing your own kind. Didn't seem to bother our boss much. She killed others like it was her job or something."

Holly hid her laugh. This girl was young. She couldn't have been much older than a teenager. And she sounded like one too. Holly turned to Alexander. She smiled at him when he took a step back when Phil growled.

"Don't mind him. He's my mate." He didn't move, nor did Phil. "How old are you both? You can't be very old."

"I'm twenty-five," he answered her. "Those two there are eighteen, and Daniel and Corey are nineteen. She took them about three weeks ago. The girl next to them, her name is Lisa and she is twenty. She had the misfortune of wandering into the building where we were and the boss took her about a week ago. And that young man is nineteen. I don't remember his name. She picked him up last night. Shelly here is the youngest at sixteen."

Lisa stayed on the ground. She looked so bad that Holly wanted to offer her her wrist. She knew that she couldn't, but it didn't make her want to do it any less. She looked away when the girl looked up at her.

"Can you change us back?" She scrubbed her hand over her face to wipe at the tears. "I had a life. A home and a boyfriend. He wasn't the greatest boyfriend in the world, but he was mine. I want to go back to my life."

Phil kneeled down to her and Holly had the overwhelming urge to snarl. Sheesh, what a mood swing. One second she wanted to help her, the next she wanted to kill her. She took several steps back when she heard Phil speak to her.

"I'm sorry, Lisa, but we cannot. She made you into a vampire and there isn't a way to change you back. There is help you can—"

"I don't want any fucking help. I want to be human again not this…this monster." The girl stood up and backed away. "Do you have any idea what it's like? What it feels like to want to grab the first thing that gets close enough to you to drain them? Every second of every hour of every day, a constant hunger burns at you? My God, I went to see Howard and all I could think about was how much his blood was making my mouth water, how much I wanted to throw him to the floor and rip his throat out. I want to die."

"Stop," Phil shouted. "Right now. You can control this with time and training. And as for the hunger, that too can be taken care of. There are places that will take you in and feed you. Show you how to take care of yourself. You can make this work for you."

"No, I can't," the girl said softly. "I have no desire to." And with that, she disappeared into the woods. When Holly started to go after her, Phil stopped her.

"Rolland is on her trail. He'll help her. There are places that…you all will be taken to a place where you'll get the training you need, help."

The forest seemed to light up for several seconds and with the dimming, Holly had her gun out and was standing in front of the younger ones. Before she could react, her brother suddenly sprang up and growled low. There were ten men and women standing in the field around them.

"These people are our trainers. They will take you with them and help you all. No more harm will come to you." Phil looked around as he continued. "Don't worry about Lisa. When she's ready to accept, she'll be brought with you."

"I'd like to stay. I'd like to...there's someone I want to find. A man by the name of Clint Burris. I'd like to find him." Alexander turned to Phil. "I...I've figured out what he is and I think I can help him in his work now. He said I had a place with him."

Phil looked at Holly. "The doctor you had in the hospital. The one that has joined your pack. What do you think?"

She didn't get a chance to answer as her brother took that moment to shift. "I think that would be a great idea. But only if you work with Phil here too. He's my friend and he'll...if he's willing, he'll get you on the right path." He looked at Phil when he growled. "You owe me, buddy. This will make us about even."

"Like bloody hell it will. You owe me more than your fat ass can pay." Phil looked at her while he spoke to her brother. "But I'll call it even if you tell me that you'll leave us alone for a long week. Holly and I have some catching up to do."

She shivered. Her entire body was on fire for the man in front of her. When she stepped up to him and wrapped her arms around him, she could hear her brother cussing and Alexander laughing. As they left the area for wherever Phil was taking them, she thought she heard her brother telling Alexander that his day was coming too.

The room he took her to was one she'd never seen before. Not that she had a lot of time to look around. She was naked before she hit the bed and Phil was inside of her scant seconds later. She screamed her first of what she was sure would be many climaxes before she had a chance to ask him anything.

"Again. Come for me again, love. I need to feel it before I can come inside of you." Even as her body lifted again she knew that she'd never get enough of him. Not just the sex, but his love. As her third then fourth peak took her, Holly screamed that she loved him, loved Phil for all of time and then some.

CHAPTER 17

They spent three days in bed. Phil wasn't sure if it was a record or anything, but he certainly felt like it was. He was going down the stairs to his kitchen to fix Holly a much needed breakfast when his cell phone rang. He groaned when he saw who it was.

"Rolland, I told you not to bother me unless—"

"She's dead. She met the sun this morning. I had her in one of the cells until last night, but she asked to see her friend Shelly. I didn't know, Phil. I'm so sorry, I had no idea."

Lisa had killed herself. If Phil was honest with himself, he knew that she would have done it anyway. He sat in the kitchen chair and talked with his brother. "She was set on it anyway, I think. I doubt there was anything you could have done to change her mind."

He thought about the vibrant young girl and wondered how the others were taking it. "She was going to see Shelly. How is she taking it, and the others? Are they okay?"

He heard Holly coming down the stairs. He thought she'd felt his pain. He'd forgotten to hide it from her. Then he felt guilty. She'd known the girl too, and he knew she'd want to know. He pulled her into his lap and held her as Rolland continued.

"Shelly is taking it the hardest. I think the others knew it was only a matter of time. They've all filed charges against their maker. Even Lisa." Rolland took a deep breath and Phil knew that whatever it was, he wasn't going to be happy about it. His brother continued. "The rogue is claiming she is wrongly accused. Not that anyone believes her, but you know how they can be. The Trustees, I mean."

"I know. Is...where is Anye?" Phil let Holly go when she stood and went to the fridge. He was momentarily distracted when she bent over into it. Christ, he was hard that fast. He heard his brother speaking and realized that he'd lost his train of thought.

"Phil, are you listening? I said, where is she? I didn't know you knew where they'd taken her. I don't."

"I thought that.... Jose Benson took her to the cells. He said he was going to take care of her." He frowned, trying to think just what he'd said. "He said that he was going to kill her for her crimes."

"I haven't seen Jose for about a month now. I thought I'd heard...let me ask Mom." Phil started pacing as he waited for his brother to come back. Something was off. And he was sure that Anye was as free as he was. "Jose left the Trustees about three months ago. Mom said he and some woman had taken up together and that no one knew who she was. If he took Anye—"

"Mother fuck," Phil shouted, and earned a raised brow from Holly. "She is free. Jose took her away and lied to me. When I get my hands on that bastard, I'm going to skin them both alive." He hung up with his brother and reached out to the other Trustees. There were supposed to be five of them, making it so that there was an uneven spread across the system. The first person he was able to contact confirmed what his brother had said.

"Yes. We never did figure it out. It would have been easier if we didn't have the hard set rule about taking the blood of each other. But Jose left some time ago. I'm not sure where he was headed; he'd mentioned that he wanted to go somewhere where it wasn't dark." The Trustee laughed. "Why he'd want to go where the sun was always shining was beyond me."

After thanking her he sat down again. Holly setting a plate of breakfast in front of him made him look up at her. There were ten slices of bacon, five sausage links, and a pile of fried ham. There were at least a dozen eggs and a half pound of fried potatoes. She had a plate in front of her filled just as full. There was a plate of toast and a crock of butter set down next. He had a fleeting thought that one of her brothers was coming to eat with them, or possibly all of them.

"Will I be able to feed you all the time?" he asked as she tucked into her food. Her laughter was what he'd hoped for. "I meant to come down and fix this for you. I'm sorry."

"Don't be. I had fun and I know you were working something out." She handed him a glass of milk. "I have to go to the office today. I have to figure out what's going on."

He started eating and stopped when she mentioned her office. She wasn't going in alone and he told her so.

"I know that. In fact, I was counting on you going with me. Also, you need to be aware that…well, I'm thinking about quitting." He looked at her. Surely she couldn't be….

When she started laughing, Phil stood up, pulled her into his arms, and kissed her.

He picked her up and she wrapped her legs around his waist. He wanted her again and right now. Swiping his hand over the table and clearing it of the remnants of their breakfast, he laid her on it. He was glad now that he'd not taken the time to put on a shirt, especially since she was wearing it and nothing else.

"I need my dessert. And you're just the thing I need." He pulled the chair around, set it between her legs, and sat down. "Perfect. Just perfect."

Pulling her forward, he lifted her thighs so that they lay over his shoulders. He was going to feast on her and he didn't want anything to get in his way. He reached up her thighs and tore her panties from her.

"You should know that I love tearing these things from you. I think you'll need to start buying in bulk. That way we won't have to worry about how many we shred." He licked her inner thigh and kissed her knee. "Of course, you could go without them. I'm not sure how practical that would be when you are wearing pants, but for me, it would save time."

"You are talking entirely too much. Shut up and eat me or let me suck you." He grinned when she growled. "I mean it, Phil."

He leaned into her and licked her from gate to clit. Christ, she tasted delicious. He took another lick at her before he pulled her closer to him, slid his finger into her, and pulled her nubbin into his mouth. She was so tight and wet that he didn't have any trouble fucking her like this. When she began riding his mouth, lifting her ass up to meet him, he inserted another finger into her heat and started fucking her with his tongue too.

You have no idea how delicious you taste to me. When you come, and you will, I'm going to drink your nectar and then I'm going to ram my cock deep into this hot, sweet pussy. Her climax rolled over him. He took as much of her cream into his mouth as he could before he slid his fingers out and into her ass. Tight. *Soon I'm going to take you here and when I do, I'm going to pink up this beauty before I fill you with my cum.*

He stood up when she came again. He tore his pants open and rubbed his thick cock over her opening, not touching her clitoris. Her begging made him pause, more because he didn't want to come all over her than that he wanted to prolong this. Finally, he moved just the thick head into her.

"Please. I'm begging you, please fill me. Phil, please." Slowly, he entered her and every inch he moved, he could feel her walls grab him, stroke him, until he knew it was only a matter of time before he exploded in her.

Moving with care and trying his best not to slam into her like he wanted, he opened her legs wider and looked down at them. She was soaking him. Not only that, but his cock glistened with her juices, and they ran down and pooled on the table beneath her. Taking several deep breaths as he moved even slower, he watched how her pussy fit around him, how with each inward movement she seemed to suck him in. He moved deeper still, until he was fully in her to his balls. He stopped moving.

She sat up, her eyes dazed and dark. He knew that he loved her, had for a long time, but seeing her like this, spread beneath him naked, he fell in love with her more.

"I love you, Holly Force Campbell. I've never loved anyone, nor will I ever love anyone, as much as I do you right now." She sat up on her elbows and looked at him. "You've no idea how long I've waited for you. You've no idea...I need you more than my next breath."

She sat up and he lifted her so that she was wrapped around him again. When he turned and sat in the chair, she settled over his cock by wrapping her legs around the back of the chair and held him to her. Lifting her breast, she fed it to him.

"Drink from me here. I want to feel you suckle my breast and drink." Her voice was deep, husky, and full of emotion.

When she pulled him closer to her as he took her nipple into his mouth, she begged again for him to bite. He sank his fangs deep.

She screamed out her release. He felt her move up and down over his hips in a frenzied movement. He felt his balls tighten up and knew that he was going to come. Licking the wounds closed, he stood and took them both to the floor. Never letting go of her, he started slamming into her as soon as her back touched the tile.

When he came he knew that never had a release been so fulfilling. Never had he felt every drop of his cum pass through him and into someone else. His body still reeling, his climax grabbed him again and he felt another powerful one pour from him. He nuzzled her neck, feeling her do the same to him, and he bit her again as he heard her screaming against his skin. He was going to pass out, he thought. He was simply going to faint like a young girl.

He woke with a blanket over him. He had no idea how long he'd lain there, but he was sure it had only been seconds. But he knew as soon as he stood it had been longer. The dishes where cleaned up and the rest of the kitchen was just as clean. There was a note on the chalkboard near the refrigerator.

Hope you slept well. I tried to wake you several times and finally gave up. I've never known anyone to sleep so hard.

I had to go out. I'm meeting CJ at the mall. She wants to get out of the house and I need to get a handle on getting bulk panties ~ Christ, you're hard on a girl's clothes. Anyway, see you around three.

I love you,
Holly Campbell (Don't you just love the way that sounds?)

He didn't like her going out without him, but he had obviously needed the rest. It had been awhile since he'd slept so well and so long. Stretching, he went to the bathroom to grab a shower and change. Or in this case, dress. He gathered up the bits and pieces of his pants and went to shower.

Twenty minutes later he walked into the kitchen, and was surprised to find Austin at his back door with a woman he'd not seen in a while, Stacy O'Brien. She didn't look all that thrilled to be there, and Phil understood why when she was followed in by Dallas. He wondered if the man had figured it out yet. But when he continued with a conversation they'd likely been having outside his house, he realized he hadn't.

"There is no reason for you to get snippy with me. I'm just pointing out that you'd be better off if you stay out of a relationship with a wolf you've only known for a few months and keep yourself free. You've no idea what kind of person he is."

"I will live where I want and with who I want. Just stay the fuck away from me and out of my business." She grinned at Phil. "He thinks because I happen to come around and help CJ out that he has some sort of power over me. He's just an ass as far as I'm concerned."

Phil liked the wolf. He knew from CJ and Alexis that she'd had some hard times, but she seemed to be stronger for them. When he turned to Austin, the man was dipping into his refrigerator like he owned it. He flushed when he turned to Phil with a beer in his hand.

"CJ won't let me have any in the house. She said that the babies might get into them by mistake." He took a long pull on the dark brew. "I have no idea how they're going to manage that since they're only two weeks old. But I love her and let her have her way. For now. I'm supposed to meet her here in half an hour."

As he sat down Phil got another beer for Stacy and sat with them. Dallas declined, but got himself a glass of tea instead.

It was nearly four o'clock and Phil was starved. Standing again, he pulled ten steaks out of the freezer and told Dallas to get the potatoes.

"I take it you guys won't mind staying for dinner?" That question met with hearty approval, so he had Stacy pull out stuff for a salad.

"We won't eat it, so unless you want me to simply cut up some of this green crap and put it on a plate for you, I'm not going to waste my time." Phil handed her a knife and told her to cut. "Your food."

He knew that CJ ate salad and he could stomach it if necessary, but he didn't tell the bitch that. He grinned when he thought about her being a bitch and wondered how many other species named their females such an appropriate name.

He was just looking at his watch when his and Austin's cell phones went off. He knew the moment that Austin fell into the chair that something horrible had happened. He answered his own phone, knowing that his mate wasn't at the other end.

"They took her. Right out from the changing booth." CJ was talking calmly, but he knew she was on edge. "Come here with me before I have to kill this stupid cop. And for the love of Peter, bring Dallas. This moron has it in his head that she's run away and she'll turn up when she's good and ready." Phil leaned against the counter and took a deep breath. CJ was still talking. "—at the north entrance near the food court. Are you still there?"

"Yes. Yes, I'm still here. I'm going to meet you at the north entrance. Are you standing there now?" She confirmed that she was. "Don't move. I have you and I don't want to bump into anyone else when I get there."

"Phil, I'm so sorry. This was my idea. I needed to get out and I don't have any female friends and I just—"

Phil was suddenly there. His magic to move quickly like he could made it possible, and for the first time in ages, he was glad for this one ability. He took the phone from her and closed it. He held her while she cried and wondered if he could tell her to buck up and go to where his Holly had been. She seemed to get herself under control and led him to the boutique around the corner, talking a mile a minute as she walked.

"We were going to surprise you with a naughty nightie. Well, she was. I was simply talking her into it. She said you got all manly with her clothes and maybe you'd slow down if she bought you something sexy. I didn't see the logic in that, but she seemed to think it would work." She took a deep breath. "I'm babbling, aren't I? I do that when I'm scared. Or nervous. I think I'm both. She's my sister-in-law, I know, but I love her like we're really of blood. I suppose we are if you—"

He laid his hand over her mouth. "I'm sorry, love, but I need answers. If I take my hand away, can you answer only them? I promise I'll let you babble the next time." She nodded then burst into tears.

"I'm so sorry." He held her again as they moved into what looked like a nightmare.

Police tape was everywhere. He didn't understand why there was so much of it until he really looked. Displays were knocked over and clothes shredded. There was broken glass on the trashed clothing and he spied a nightie that made him think of Holly. There was a sticky substance on the floor and some of the walls, and it took him several seconds to realize it was blood. He looked at CJ when she sobbed.

"She fought so hard to save those two women. They were screaming so...she even tried to reason with her, but she kept laughing at her. I thought…I actually thought to contact you both, but there was some sort of block on me."

"She held your mind. Holly's too. She is Anye, she was here. She has Holly." He walked over to a covered body. He nodded to the cop and it took him several seconds to realize it was Connor. He took back the sheet.

The woman, a young girl really, had had her throat ripped out. She'd bled out so quickly that even if a paramedic had been standing next to her, he wouldn't have been able to save her. Her throat was literally gone. He moved to the other sheet and saw that this girl's chest had been torn in much the same fashion as the other one. Her heart was exposed and while not beating now, Phil could see that it had been exposed while still moving. He covered both women up and stood. That's when he saw the paramedics working.

"It's that cop, the one that's been helping you. They don't think he's going to make it. He'd been in the wrong place at the wrong time."

Phil rushed to him. He slid into the mind of all of EMTs and had them move back. Myles heart was nearly stopped. He either acted now or the man would die. Phil kneeled down and leaned to Myles's head. "I'm so sorry, my friend, but I can't let you go this way. I need you too much. Not just for this, but for your friendship." Phil opened his vein at his wrist and lay it over the dying man's mouth. "Drink from me. Take into you my life and live as a shadow of the darkness. Stand as my child, learn from me."

He didn't need to say the words to convert the man, but he felt comfort in them. Phil was afraid he was too late when his life giving blood slipped down his chin. When a hand suddenly appeared and held Myles's nose, he was surprised to see Austin there.

Neither of them said a word as the man drank. When they could see that he was getting stronger, Phil took his wrist away and sealed the wound. He had to find his Holly.

"He won't die. My brother and parents are coming to watch over him. But I can't...I have to find her." Austin stood too, anger in every pore of his body. "I'll find her. You have to believe me."

"I do. And if you think this bitch is taking part of my family and I'm going to sit idly by, then you're as nutty as a fruitcake. Tell me where her scent is the strongest and I'll have all I have to help you."

He should have expected the hug. He'd been around these wolves enough to know that hugging was as much a part of them as taking a breath. When he could stand on his own after having all the wind squeezed out of him, he pointed to the counter.

Austin went to the counter. Then he looked around the room to be sure no one was watching. Phil watched as the alpha shifted, his muzzle appearing as he leaned down and took a deep breath of the scents Phil knew were there. When something touched his leg, he looked down to see Myles staring at him.

"Don't speak. You've been hurt badly." He touched the man's hand, which now lay over his chest. "I'm going to...to change you. Do you understand?"

Phil saw the confusion and didn't make any effort to clear it up. He didn't want to have to explain what was going to happen nor did he have the time. When Myles opened his palm, Phil looked at it.

"Him," Myles whispered. "Him."

There was a small scrap of material in his hand. He started to reach for it when his hand closed again. Phil reached into Myles mind and settled it before he could speak to him.

Him? You mean there was a man here with Anye? Can you let me see what he looked like? Phil searched through his memories and with it, the man's emotions and pain. I'm so sorry, my friend. You shouldn't have had to deal with them.

Myles had been shopping for a baby gift. He'd been looking for something to give to CJ and Austin's new babies when he'd seen her walk into the little store with Holly. He walked in just as Holly shot at the older vampire. The girl at the counter was already dead and Jose was feeding from the one that now lay on the floor.

"Myles, get back," he'd been told by CJ. He looked toward her and saw her standing near the far wall. She looked frozen there to him, but the first bullet hit him in the shoulder. He looked at Holly to see why she'd shot him, when another bullet hit him in the belly. Pain tore at him, yet he knew that if he went down, he'd be more of a hindrance than help, so he pulled his own gun and shot at the vampire. Holly didn't have her gun pointed at him but at the woman.

Myles never got the chance to fire. Jose suddenly had him lifted up and before he could do whatever it was he'd planned, Anye spoke.

"He's a buddy of Phil's. Don't kill him, but do make it so he will die. I want the bastard to suffer like he did me. Just...I don't know, mess him up really bad in the guts. That will be painful to the prick too."

"You telling me how to do my job? I got news for you, I've been messing people up for a long time. In fact, it's sort of a hobby of mine." The laughter made the skin on Phil's arms crawl. "You should try to get this over with soon, love; the cops are on their way."

Jose had turned Myles in his arms and slammed him several times against the wall. Phil could feel each time he hit as though he was the victim instead of his friend. Pulling out of his mind, Phil put Myles to sleep and contacted his mother again.

He'll need to be fed again. I can't...I have to save my strength in case Holly needs me.

You go. I'm nearly there. I've brought your brother with me too. Rolland is going with you and your father. But the others will help with— He felt her sob. Bring her back whole, Phil. I really like this girl.

Phil didn't take the material, but lifted Myles's hand to his nose. He could smell them, both men on it. But what he hadn't expected was the blood. Moving the material, he saw a small drop of blood there so he leaned down and licked it. It wasn't anyone he'd drank from before and knew it had to be Jose. He had him now.

CHAPTER 18

Holly couldn't move very much and when she did, it was nearly painful enough to make her want to black out. She peered around the small box she was in and tried to think about anything other than the fact that she knew she was in a coffin.

It was lined with silver. If she reached up to touch the lid she got burned. She'd learned that the hard way. The padding under her wasn't very thick and she knew that if she tried to move too much, it would fall through. Holly thought that if the bedlike cot she was lying on were to fall to the bottom of the casket, she could land on something that would kill her.

Then there was her throat. The bite wasn't big. She'd only been bitten enough that she bled. Holly tried to seal it with her own saliva, but all it did was burn a little and nothing more. Blood was pouring from her, too much for her to live much longer if she didn't get help. Holly reached for Phil and hit a wall. Then she thought that she was in a steel room or underground. Holly so didn't want to think of that right now.

The lid opening suddenly made her flinch. The sudden light burned her eyes, and before she could focus on whatever had unearthed her, she was being tossed against a wall.

"There she is just like I told you. Didn't I tell you that I'd get her for you? Now you owe me big time. When can I expect payment?"

Holly didn't say anything as Anye crowed.

"You said she was a wolf. All I see is the bitch that was getting my job. There isn't any earthly reason for me to pay you if all I got is a stupid female."

Holly knew that voice. She turned slightly to see how he was involved and saw her boss, Eli Blair, there.

"Don't look at me like you didn't know. I've been trying to kill you off for months."

"Why?" she whispered. Her throat hurt more when she spoke so she decided to do it as little as possible. Trying to stand made her dizzy, but the look on his face was worth every pain she had to endure. He was terrified of her.

"Why? Are you fucking nuts? Of course you are. You had to die because I hate competition. You, my dear, were better than me, and I just can't stand that. Especially when it's a woman." He started pacing. "Do you have any idea how much ribbing I endured because of you? How much the men admired you for your skills? Shit, it was like they were ready to build a fucking statue to you. I couldn't stand it anymore, and when that last assignment didn't get you killed...." He shrugged. "I took matters into my own hands and tried to find someone who knew you. That's when this bitch showed up."

"He's going to use you and abuse you," Anye said gleefully. "He and I have worked out a deal where I'm going to keep you for a while, until Phil shows up, then I'll heal you and you will belong to him. See? Everyone is happy."

Except for her. Holly tried to reach for Phil again, and nothing. Now she was getting scared. Not only that, but she was reasonably sure that whatever Blair's plans for her were, they didn't involve her going back to work for him. Holly tried to think. Dizziness wasn't just an occasional thing now but a constant reminder that she was dying. Holly thought about letting them think she passed out, but was afraid of the reality of it. They would kill her if she did.

"Shift for him. I know you can, I've seen you do it. Shift for him and let him see you are a wolf." Anye kicked her in the ribs then backed away before Holly could grab her. "Shift, bitch, now."

Holly knew that if she shifted, she'd be a wolf for an hour, no less. She also knew that the wound at her neck would heal, but she was very weak so it would only slow her down, not help. Then something occurred to her. Austin and Dallas. If she shifted, no matter where she was, they could hear her. She stood up by sliding against the wall for support.

"She leaves. I don't do tricks and she's a fucking bitch." Anye lunged at Holly, but she grabbed her by the neck and tossed her away. It cost her a great deal and she tried her best not to show it.

Blair stared at her for several seconds. When almost a minute went by he finally spoke. "Leave us."

"She is trying to get us to separate so she can try and kill us one at a time. Don't you see?" Anye let her beast go and it made Holly's snarl along her skin. This was not good.

"I said leave us. I'm the one with the money. Besides, I have a gun with silver in it and I'm not opposed to killing her." He pulled the gun and looked at her until Anye left the room. Of course, she did kick Holly once again. The door closed with a click.

"You won't get away with this. They know who you are and will be able to find you without any problems." She didn't move toward him. She was sure she could get to him before he fired, but wasn't going to take the chance.

"Is that how you became so good? Using your special powers to find your targets? I would imagine that it was so easy for you." He nodded to the floor. "Sit down."

She slid to the floor but stayed on her feet. She wanted to be able to move when she needed to. She waited for him to tell her to shift again. When he did, she let her beast go.

The power was immediate. Her entire body surged with it. As soon as she felt her wolf fully out, she reached for her brother.

Austin, you have to find Phil now. I'm in big fucking trouble here and I think that this slimy bastard is going to shoot me.

~~~

Austin stopped pacing and grabbed him. Phil thought the man was in pain, but when he turned to look at him with the most heinous smile, Phil took a step back.

"I have her. She's shifted and is telling me to get to you." Austin grabbed a sheet of paper and a pen from the counter and began writing things down. Phil leaned in and started reading the cryptic notes.

Coffin. Blair. Bitch Anye. Walls of steel and silver dust. Superman???

Austin turned to him and looked worried. "She said she's bleeding at her neck that she thinks Anye did it to have her die slowly. She wants to know what to do."

"Tell her to seal it with her saliva and—" Austin was already shaking his head. "She tried that, I take it. Tell her that her blood should heal her if she simply cut...wait, you said she had shifted. Wouldn't that take care of it?"

He had no idea. There were things he knew about wolves and packs, but really not a lot about how they healed. He looked at Austin as he shook his head again.

"A bite won't heal if it's from a vamp. Not sure why, but there you have it. I told her about the blood. She said when she shifts back, she'll try it. But she said to tell you to get your ass to her. She needs your Superman suit."

Superman suit? Phil was pacing when something else occurred to him. She was speaking to her brother but not him. Steel walls would have blocked him. Blair meant her boss was there. He was more than likely working with his company to have her eliminated. But that really didn't make any sense either. Superman suit. Then it hit him.

"My armor. She needs my armor. Guns. There are guns there and Blair is trying to…fuck. How do I get to her? Can you find her?" Austin nodded then shook his head. "Which is it, big boy, my patience is about at its end."

"I can find her, but only so far. If I can get you to where I think she is then you'll have to find her yourself. I can track as a wolf, but that's not help much in a steel room with silver dust. It will kill me and her if she inhales it." Austin took off his shirt and handed it to him. "My pack is coming. Connor will take care of this mess for us and your buddy Myles is headed to my house. There's a basement addition we had put in for you to visit."

Phil didn't register much other than he was going to find his mate. He nodded absently and then turned to Connor. He needed to make sure there was someone there when Holly was brought home. He didn't want just anyone taking care of her.

"I will have Clint there. I know you don't fully trust him, but he is my friend. I knew him from…it's been a long time, but I trust him." Connor stepped closer. "I also have taken in your new friend Alexander. He's been checked out. Also, there is a missing person's report on him that I'm taking care of. Luckily, he has no one looking for him other than another vet. I think it'll be easy to have him die, don't you?"

Phil nodded. He didn't particularly care for the vamp, but he had helped Austin and Holly. He turned around when the room seemed to expand around them. Austin was standing in the doorway to the back room as a huge wolf.

The wolf didn't go unnoticed, but Phil was able to take care of the scare he'd caused. Once he and Dallas got Austin to the car and in the back, they took off in the direction that he'd said he had to go. When he slowed at a stop sign, Austin came up front and clawed at the window. Phil lowered it and the big wolf leaned out.

If the situation wasn't so grave, Phil might have laughed. He was driving down the road with this big fucking dog hanging out the window with his tongue hanging out and his face flapping in the wind. He chuckled when he glanced at Dallas in the rearview mirror.

"If you're thinking what I think you're thinking, I'd not say it out loud. He is very touchy about his appearance."

"Why is he doing it then?" Phil turned left when Austin barked twice. It was a system that he'd worked out with him before they knew Dallas was coming along.

"He can smell her. Even if you take him hundreds of miles from home, if he can ride like he is now, he can get back. Dogs are much the same way. It's why when people take their dogs out into the woods and drop them off, some of them return. They get the scents on their tongue and can simply go in reverse."

Phil decided that when this was over, he was going to sit down with this pack and learn all he could. He was family now and he thought he should know. He turned right at the next intersection when Austin barked again. Dallas's phone ringing startled them both.

"Fuck," he said when he closed the phone. "That was Gordon. He's taking Alexis into the hospital. She's in labor. She couldn't wait one more day, could she?"

Phil laughed. "No, she couldn't. But hers and Gordon's child will be a blessing when this is finished."

Phil turned when Austin indicated, then stopped the car when Dallas told him to. He went around and opened the door for the big animal, and waited while he sniffed around. He was about ready to yell at the stupid mutt when he went to the same area three times until he took off running. Phil went with him. He could hear Dallas close behind.

They ended up in the middle of a field. There was nothing; no tire marks, no house, nothing to indicate that Holly was anywhere close to them. She could be anywhere. He closed his eyes and reached for her and felt the smallest of connections.

"She's here. Somewhere...I don't know how close, but here." He dug deeper, reached further, and found her again. He turned to Dallas when he cleared his throat. He turned to his left when he was suddenly knocked down. He started to throw Austin off when he heard a sound.

It was Anye. She was standing in the field not twenty feet away from them. He hadn't seen where she came from, but if she was here then they were on the right path. He watched as she disappeared and still Austin didn't move. It wasn't until Dallas stood over them that Austin moved off him.

"Did you see where she came from?" Dallas asked. Phil shook his head. "We can track her. If she came on foot. I know you vamps have a mode of travel that we don't have. It's hard to track—"

Phil hit the ground, covering his head with his hands. Holly. It was Holly and she screamed for him. He looked at Austin when he whimpered. "She screamed for me. We have to find her now. She is in a great deal of pain."

CHAPTER 19

He'd shot her, the fucking bastard. Baring her teeth at him made her want to latch her canines around his neck and snap it. She would, too, if she ever got the chance. This sucker was a dead man.

"You have one more minute before I shoot you again. Now shift or whatever it is you do to make yourself human again. I have to get you out of here and I think you're a bit stronger than me in your current body." He grinned at her again. "Of course, you will have to learn to obey me in either form, but just so you know, I'm going to take great pleasure in making you obey my every command."

He rubbed his cock again. He'd been hard since she'd shifted. She wondered if the guy had an animal fetish and decided that there were some things she just didn't want to know. Pacing close to the wall, she whimpered. Just as he raised his gun again, Holly felt Phil coming. She only hoped it wasn't too late.

The bullet ripped through her front flank. She knew that had he hit her where he was aiming, he would have killed her. Didn't the guy have a fucking clue where her heart was? She whimpered again, this time to cover the sounds coming from above. Phil was crashing through whatever was above them like a demolition crew.

"This is the last time I'm going to tell you, bitch. Change back or I'm going to end this relationship I was forming right fucking now." He waved the gun at her just as she heard Phil on the other side of the door.

"It ends now." Phil crashed through the door just as the gun went off. If the bullet hit him, he didn't show it.

Blair was suddenly in pieces. Not big ones either, but small bits of him all over the room. When his gun slid toward her, she simply stared at it. There was no way he'd ever be using it again. When Phil knelt before her she scooted back. Not that she was afraid of him, but she was hurting and she was afraid.

"Come on, baby. Let me lift you up. I need to get you out of here before Anye returns. And your brothers are still a bit behind me." She was being lifted when suddenly, she was being dropped again. Before she could ask him, she saw why.

"You should have moved a little faster, Phil. But I do not appreciate you killing my friend over there before I got my money. However, now I have two bargaining chips. You and the bitch." Anye moved into the room and looked over at her. "She'll be dead soon enough. There is no way that a wolf can heal from a wound from a vampire."

Phil wondered how she knew that and thought of Jose. Okay, this meeting between him and the pack was becoming more and more necessary. But he glanced at Holly before he continued.

"She won't die from the bite, dumbass. She's my mate and I bite her daily." He was bluffing and hoped she didn't have an answer for that too. "As a matter of fact, before you became stupid, or should I say stupider, we were just going over her training for her to do all sorts of things I can do."

Another lie, but again, he didn't think she knew. He leaned back against the wall and reached for Holly. He was trying his best to keep Anye occupied until Holly could move out of the small cavern.

Leave here and find your brothers. Send them to me as soon as you're safe. I can—

Don't be fucking stupid. I'm not leaving you. I'm just getting my second wind. Let's kill this bitch. He could hear her lie for what it was and loved her all the more for it, but she had to get out before Jose returned.

Holly, I'm ordering you to leave here now. As soon as the words left his mouth, he knew he'd made a mistake. She didn't take orders any better than his friend CJ. Worse, he would imagine.

Her snarl made them both look at her. The sight of her standing there as a full-grown wolf would forever be burned into his mind. She looked like an avenging angel and one pissed off bitch. He turned and shifted to his knight as soon as he saw Jose join in the fray.

He stepped to Anye and brushed against her. He knew she was aware of what would happen, but by the time he was going for Jose, she was already screaming. Phil lunged at Jose just as he saw a blur of fur going after the vampire. Phil was never so grateful in his entire life to see Austin.

"You fucking prick. Why couldn't you have just left us alone? All we wanted was to get some money and leave. Now look what you've made us do."

Phil grinned. "Me? No, the moment you touched what was mine, you sealed your fate. I take my role as a mate very seriously. You should have left when you had the chance. Now, well, now you're going to join the other prisoners in the cells below the castle keep."

Jose pulled a sword from the air. He waved it in front of Phil several times before he spoke again. "I'm not going anywhere with you. You are going to let me walk away and when you do, I might let your bitch live. But I'm not making any sort of promises."

Phil wasn't worried. His armor would keep him safe and the sword that Jose had now was nothing more than a stainless steel blade, and not a very good one at that. He did worry about Holly, though. She was still hurt and—

He looked behind him just as another scream came from Anye. It wasn't Austin like he'd assumed, but Holly. Christ, she was the most stubborn woman he'd ever—

The blade hit him in the chest. The sparks sprayed over Jose and him, but did little to nothing to either man. But the other man knew that he wasn't going to penetrate his shield so easily. He stepped back and seemingly pulled another blade from the air as the first one disappeared.

"Steel doesn't work, but that's fine. I have a whole arsenal here that I can keep banging away at you with until I find a good one." This time, when the blade came at him, Phil leapt forward. He grabbed Jose by the throat.

"I don't have that kind of time." Another scream rent the air and Phil snapped Jose's neck. It wouldn't kill him, but it would slow him down a bit. Just as he turned to help Holly, Austin entered the small room.

"Take him. But don't let his blood touch you. It's poison because of his position in the Trustees." Phil moved to Holly and Anye. "Holly, love, you have to come away from her."

She growled low in her throat and Phil hoped that as his mate, even in her pain-riddled body, she'd not be able to hurt him. He dropped to his knees as he shifted to his regular street clothes.

Holly had Anye by the throat. The vampire was still alive, but not by much. She was bleeding out quickly and Phil knew that if she died this way, they might never figure out why she'd done it. Not that it mattered, he supposed, but he would like to know why she'd betrayed her entire race.

"Holly Campbell, let her go. Now." The compulsion in Austin's voice was hard to miss. Phil had the feeling that the alpha rarely used that tone and, if he did, he got results. Holly whimpered once again and let the woman go. She shifted almost immediately so that her wounds would heal, he assumed.

"Thank you. Now, Anye, you are hereby ordered by the High Trustees of Vampires to be brought before them in trial. You'll be imprisoned until such time that—"

"You can't do this to me. I'm not some nobody that you can take to prison like a common criminal. I demand that you take me to be healed, then we'll see about where I'll go from there." She stood up, bit her wrist, and rubbed it over her neck. Then when she had that taken care of, she straightened up her clothing. No one spoke as she did this.

"You finished primping?" Holly laughed. "Christ, you'd think you were on your way to a tea party and not your own death."

Phil laughed too. He couldn't help it. He was standing in a room covered in blood and gore with a vampire who lay behind him with a boot at his broken neck and one in front of him that was fixing her hair. He had a naked...no, make that two naked wolves standing around him and one at the door laughing as well.

"I do not think there is anything funny about this. You may take me to my office now. I'm quite ready to explain what happened here today." Anye looked over at Holly and grinned.

"I always knew that you'd be trouble. When I'm finished speaking, you'll wish you'd never met me."

Holly stood up and was handed a shirt by Dallas. Then a man was handing his brother some clothes as well. He'd have to remember to thank the wolf later.

"You think I don't already wish I'd never met you? Honey, you have no idea how true that statement is." The shirt covered most of her body, but to Phil, it was still too short. "Phil, why don't you deliver this bitch to her cell and I'll meet you back at the house?"

He nodded to Dallas, who came forward and stood in front of Anye. That was when Phil noticed that he had on a pair of thick gloves and a silver chain in his hands. Phil laughed again.

"You wolves? Are you always so prepared?"

Dallas laughed as he wrapped the chain around Anye's waist and wrists. No amount of her screaming made him remove them. "Connor handed me this pack before I left the mall. He said that I'd probably need it, but I had to refill it when I gave it back to him." Dallas held the chain in his hand as he slapped Anye and shut her up. "I'm thinking he might not get this back until I get a good inventory of what he packed in the sucker. Might have to make me a couple of these for myself. Whatcha think?"

Phil laughed and pulled Holly to him. "I think you might be on the right path with that. I'm taking Holly to the clinic. I will be back in a few minutes. If these two give you any trouble—"

Austin's snort cut him off. "They won't. Take her to the clinic. We'll be here when you get back."

Phil kissed Holly when she started to protest. He leaned near her ear and licked the still open wound closed. "I'm going to feed you and if I have time, fuck you. But if you protest too long, I won't have time for either."

Her mouth closed with a snap. When she wrapped her arms around him and kissed him back, he took them to the clinic. He'd completely forgotten about his family there with Myles.

He fed the human again. One more and he'd be fully vampire. The man wasn't doing as well as he'd hoped and he thought about the odds of conversion. One in every fifty survived if the human was too injured to recover. He looked over at Holly as she was brought to him.

"He needs to live. I won't let that bitch take his life just because he was at the wrong place at the wrong time." He pulled his wrist away and sealed the wounds. "I like the stupid human."

"Me too. I'll stay with him." She took Myles's hand into hers and Phil felt the stirring of his own beast. She must have felt it too. "Oh for heaven's sake, go to my brothers so they can come here to see the baby when it's born. Go."

He didn't like it, but he left. When he had time, he was going to have to tell her the rules about mates. He grinned as he walked down the stairs to where her brothers were. She more than likely knew them as well as he did.

It took them only a few minutes to gather the idiots up. Jose had healed his neck, but he was no match for a pissed off wolf. Austin had left a considerable print on his neck and Phil found himself being jealous. He and Austin put the prisoners in the separate cells in the castle, stood outside the doors, and said nothing for several minutes.

"What happens now? Do they have a trial?" He nodded toward the cell where Theresa was yelling obscenities at them both. "Will they all three be put out of our miseries?"

"Yes. They will each have their time in court, but...you don't have to worry about them getting out, Austin. Even if they did somehow manage to escape death, I'll make sure they don't ever get out."

Austin took his hand and pulled him close. "See that you do. I'd really hate to have to kick your ass over something like this." He stepped back. "Besides, I think I'll let CJ take care of you. She's a little hell cat when she's upset."

Phil laughed and was still laughing when another member of the Trustees came toward them. Phil wasn't as trusting as he had been and stood in front of the wolf and shifted.

"You're to meet with the High Council, sire. They await your...sire?"

Phil didn't move and he was glad for once that Austin didn't growl. "Who is it? The one I'm suppose to meet. Who is it?" The man looked nervous and Phil nearly felt sorry for him. "Is it someone strong enough to carry us?"

"Sire. You've been asked...she's not happy, sire. Not happy at all. She is tearing up the office as we...do you think it is possible that you hurry? Your mother...she is scary, is she not?"

Phil took a few seconds to figure out what the scribe was saying. "My mother? She's on the— good Christ, no wonder you're terrified. Take me to her. And if you want to stay on her good side...."

The man practically crawled up his arm in his attempt to beg Phil for anything to keep him on his mother's good side. "Please, sire. Anything would be most helpful. How does one stay on her good side?"

"You bring her flowers for her office and make sure she has an endless supply of books. My mother loves to read." He walked a few steps more when he gave the scribe one more piece of advice. "And whatever you do, never enter the room without knocking. My parents tend to think that any flat surface is a perfect place to have sex." Phil shuddered. He'd done that once, walked in on them in the kitchen, no less, and had not gone home in nearly a decade. And he still knocked at every doorway whether there was a door or not before he entered a room. Any room.

He knocked on the door he and Austin were shown to and walked in when given permission. His father sat on one of the chairs and his mother stood behind a massive desk throwing papers everywhere.

"I see you've made yourself at home." He kissed her cheek before he and Austin sat down. "When did this take place?"

"I'm not here as the High Council, son. I'm merely cleaning out some paperwork before the true boss shows up." She sat down behind the desk and waited. He was sure she was telling him something, but he couldn't—

"Oh no you don't," he shouted as he stood up. "I told them before that I wasn't taking this job and I'm not going to do it now. I have a mate to make love to and I want children. I'm not getting into politics again. No way."

"Too late. The moment you walked through that door, you took the position. Congratulations." She turned to Austin when he laughed. "You're not off the hook either, young man. Congratulations, you're his second."

CHAPTER 20

Phil held the tiny bundle in his arms and Holly couldn't help but marvel at how teary she was getting. Holly sat back in the chair and tried to listen to the blow by blow of what labor and delivery had been like for her sister-in-law. If she listened to Alexis, then she wouldn't be bursting into tears at any moment.

You should know that when you go into heat the next time, I plan to work very hard at impregnating you. She looked over at Phil when he spoke to her mentally. I can't wait to see you big with my child.

We haven't heard back from your mom yet. She said she didn't know if you and I could have a child. I don't want to get my hopes up too much. She wasn't entirely sure, but she thought that they couldn't have gotten much higher than they were now. She said it would take her a while.

She found an entry in the books she has. While vampires can't conceive all that often, you, my dear, are very fertile when you're in heat. She said that she didn't see any reason that we can't have plenty of babies. She felt him touch her body and she responded immediately. You keep smelling like that and we're going to have to find a dark corner or a locked closet so that I can fuck you.

Promise? Phil stood suddenly and handed the little girl to her father. She stood when he walked toward her. Where are we going?

"Home." And there they were.

The room had been redone. She remembered dark drapes on the windows before and now there were lighter ones. Before she could ask Phil about them he dropped her on the bed. She watched him unbutton his shirt.

"Shouldn't we have said something to the others before we simply left?" She licked her lips when his shirt came off. "I mean, won't they wonder where we've gone?"

"No. If they have any sense at all, they've already figured it out. Take off your clothes, Holly. I want to make love to you."

She watched as his belt joined his shirt. "Stop, please, Phil. I want to...I need to tell you something." She nearly melted when he grabbed her foot and brought it to his mouth. "Phil, you're going to...that feels so good."

He suckled on her toes. Then he moved his hands up her calves and under the skirt she had on. She swallowed three times before she could speak. But he cut her off when he touched where the elastic on her panties should have been. He froze and looked at her.

"You told me that you'd prefer I didn't wear them when I had on a dress. I know this is a skirt, but I thought you wouldn't mind." She frowned at him. "Of course if you only meant dresses, I can find some panties and put them on for you. I wouldn't want to—oof!"

He came down on top of her. His mouth was devouring hers and his hands were searing her skin with its heat. She heard her blouse rip and smiled. She supposed that making love was out of the question, that he was going to take her hard and fast. Just what she'd been hoping for.

The skirt was the next thing he ripped from her. Even as he tore at her bra, she could feel him rocking into her soft flesh between her thighs. She reached behind him and ripped his pants from his body, her claws not even scratching his skin.

He slid into her as she came. Christ, he only had to enter her and she came apart. When she felt her body start to slow she nearly screamed when he bit her nipple, bringing her to another powerful climax.

"Holly, I'm going to fuck you like this then I'm going to beat that ass of yours." He rocked into her again as he continued. "My plan was to take my time with you, make love to you slowly. You've sent me over the edge thinking about you sitting there without anything under that short skirt of yours."

She cried out again as he bit her again. "Please, you have to come in me. I need you to come inside of me, Phil, please?"

"Like this?" He stiffened over her and she felt his cum fill her sheath. "Christ," he yelled as he started fucking her harder.

Even as her body was still reeling he pulled out and flipped her over. When she got up on her knees to get away from him he slapped her ass hard. She started to snarl at him when he entered her. She laid her head down on the bed in submission as soon as he bit her shoulder.

She was going to come again. Her body was building quicker now for the crest that was just there. When he reached around her to her pussy she cried out when he flicked her clit and then he gathered her cream. When he sat up behind her, but didn't stop, she tensed when he started rubbing her tight hole.

"Don't, love. I'm not going to hurt you. I need to mark all of you. Fill this tight ass with my cum too." He rubbed harder and she felt him enter her ass with his finger. "You have no idea how much I want to fuck you here."

She didn't like the burn at first, but the longer he moved his finger in and out, the better it felt. When he moved a second finger inside of her, she moaned and he growled. The third finger slipping inside had her coming again.

"That's it, baby. Come. As soon as I slip inside of you here I'm going to bite you. I'm going to feed your ass while I drink from you." He slipped his fingers out and she whimpered. "I'm going to move slowly, baby, and you have to breathe through it. But don't tense up."

She felt his cock at her backside. She wanted to move away from him and when she did he slapped her ass. After two more hard open palms hits, she was moving back to his hand.

"More. Please, Phil, more. I want to feel you inside of me." She needed him there, she realized. Needed to feel him in her ass.

He rubbed his cock over her pussy. When he pinched her clit she came apart and flooded his cock. She could feel her juices spill from her. When he moved his cock to her ass she nearly tensed up again, but moved back instead.

It was hard work for the both of them. He would move into her an inch and then he'd still while she got used to him there. Over and over he moved into her and she took him. When she felt him lean over her and rest on her back she could feel his sweat mingle with hers. He was in her fully.

"You are so tight around me, love. I'm almost afraid to move." But he did, slowly and with care. She nearly came again when he reached around her and slid his fingers into her pussy.

"I won't last, love, so come when you want. I want to feel you come with me in you this way." She moved back when he pinched her clit. He growled at her and she moaned when he licked her shoulder. When he bit her she came apart with a scream. She felt his cum fill her even as she slid into darkness. Her last thought before she let it claim her was that she could die a happy woman.

~~~

The trial was set for nine o'clock in the evening. There were more people there than he'd thought there'd be. He'd expected ten people at the most, but nearly a hundred had shown up. He looked up at the dais and wondered who would be presiding over the courts. He smiled at his mother when she sat at his table with him.

"They said that there are some problems with the girl. Have you heard anything?" He shook his head and wondered what could be the issue. "I hope this thing doesn't last long. I've wanted to get over to the pack house and hold that little girl of Alexis's. What did she name her?"

"Allyson Gladys," Holly answered for him. She took out her cell and handed it to his mother. "They decided to call her Ally. There are about a thousand pictures of her on that along with CJ's twins. They're getting so big."

Just as his mother started going through the pictures, court was called to order. He, along with all the other people in the room, stood up and watched as a person who he presumed was a sort of bailiff came through first. He nearly fell over when his father sat himself at the high seat.

"This court recognizes the new High Trustees of Vampires as Phil R. Campbell, vampire. His second, Austin J. Force, werewolf, will take over duties when Trustee Campbell is not able. I call these proceedings to order. First on the stand."

And just like that, he was officially fucked. He glanced over at Austin who was glaring at his mother. Good luck with that, he thought. He'd been trying to get her to fix this since yesterday when they'd been bamboozled into this mess.

Theresa was brought out. She looked like she was going to some debutant dance. Her hair was piled high on her head and her dress made her look like a virginal sacrifice rather than a murderess. He thought the white dress was over the top and laughed to himself when Holly said, "oh for the love of Peter" low enough so that only the few people around them heard.

"Your honorest, I'd like to say something before you tell me that you plan to kill me." His father turned to the girl with a raised brow. "I think that I'm allowed to do that, right?"

"You can. But most people wait until the trial is over before they begin to plead their case. You thinking you might be guilty of something?" Rod Campbell turned to glare at the laughing room. "You want me to sentence the lot of you to hard labor?"

Everyone quieted down and he looked back at the girl when she cleared her throat to answer. "No, sire, I didn't do nothing wrong. I was just minding my own business when that other person bited me and turned me into this. I never had a lick of training like them people are telling me I should of. Why, I'd just lost my beau the week before or so and I just wasn't doing the things a proper girl should have."

She batted her eyes at him and Phil thought his dad's eyebrow was going to become a permanent part of his hairline. When he leaned back in his chair and regarded the girl she actually blushed. Phil sat up, not wanting to miss a moment of the show.

"So you're telling me that you were minding your own business and suddenly, for no apparent reason, somebody bites you and turns you into a vampire?" He chuckled. "Might work for some people, this innocent girly act, but I've seen your work. If you were a good girl before there'd be no reason to believe that you'd be anything different as a vamp. Sit the hell down and don't open your mouth again until I say you can. Of all the acts of…where the hell is her attorney?"

"I'm right here, your honor. I'm just here." He glared at the girl before addressing the dais. "I had only just received this client." He practically snarled the words, "This morning. After looking over the file, I've no choice but to tell you I completely agree with the court's findings and think you should—"

"Hey, you ain't supposed to do that. I want a new man. He's supposed to help me outta this mess, not help you kill me off. I want to be free. I'm just a kid who don't know no better." Theresa turned to the room. "Ain't nobody here been wanting to be free? I done those things 'cause I didn't know no better. You can't kill me. I'm going to be somebody soon."

The room was silent. It wasn't until Phil stood that someone led the girl to her table. He walked to the front of the room and addressed it. He was so glad this wasn't a human court. First of all, no one would have tolerated her standing there and secondly, he couldn't do what he was about to do.

Phil turned to the slide projector to the right of the room. He began flashing pictures of the destruction that Theresa had been made to do because she'd not had training.

"As you can see, the rogue learned fast what she could do to a human. She tore them apart in ways that had grown men puking in bushes and having difficulty holding down their food." She snickered and was hit on the head by her lawyer. Phil continued. "Over the past fifty years, she murdered humans. Murdered them in ways that made other humans question what had happened. They began to know that something was out there, someone they couldn't trust, and certainly no one they could let mainstream into their everyday lives. She has made vampires and other supernaturals alike a target for hate."

"I made people afraid of me. What do you think that felt like, you old fart? I got them to be afraid and they respected me 'cause of it."

Phil didn't say anything to her outburst.

His dad cleared his throat. "Well, I've had enough of this crap. Theresa Elizabeth Sykes, you are hereby sentenced to death. Your death will be by staking through the heart until you—"

She screamed and lunged at him. Phil didn't even try to move, but shifted so that his entire body was a lethal weapon. As soon as she came against him with her body, arms wrapped around him and her face hitting him in the chest, she leapt back. She started to scream, not in anger this time, but in pain. As the room watched, Theresa, rogue, started to have her flesh burned from her body. In a matter of a few minutes, she was dead; nothing but a white rag and a few bits of her hair remained.

CHAPTER 21

Myles sat on the bed and held his head in his hands. He swore he could hear his hair growing. There was a fly in the next county that was buzzing loud enough that his head felt as if it was splitting. He looked up through his fingers when someone opened the door. He growled at the man, and startled even himself.

"I take it the conversion didn't go too badly." Phil sat down in the chair that had Myles holding his fingers in his ears. He heard the cushions sigh loudly. "Do you have any questions?"

Myles looked up at him. "Are you fucking insane? Look at me. I'm a fucking vampire. What the hell did you do to me?"

Phil smiled and Myles thought about finding a gun and blowing the smile right off his face. He would have, too, if he wasn't afraid his eardrums would explode.

"I would have thought that much was obvious. I saved your life by making you a vamp. I think it was the best course of action considering what might have been." Phil leaned forward. "You've become very dear to my family and that of the pack. It was either save you by you becoming a vamp or a

209

werewolf. Either outcome would have been the only way you'd be here today."

Myles got up and sat back down. "I can hear a flea fart. How the hell do you get used to this shit?" He realized he was whispering and decided that he liked that better.

"You can tone it down after a bit. Don't concentrate on everything. Just listen to the sound of my voice. When you learn how to do that, it will be easier."

Myles didn't think so but he'd try anything right now. "I can't...I know that I have to...I can't bite anyone. I just...that guy that was here before, he said that I could...Christ." He'd told Myles that he was there to help him learn to feed. Myles had run him from the room when his fangs burst through his gums.

"I heard. My mother has an idea. You're my child and she thinks you should see if you can eat food. Human food. I'm having you a burger made and some fries. I'm sorry, you'll have to eat it rare, but we can see if that works for you."

Myles nodded. He'd try anything. Then what Phil said occurred to him. "I'm your kid? Because you turned me into this? Is that why?"

He could smell the food now. Meat, red and bloody. It was getting closer to him and all he could think about was biting it. He turned to Phil when he laughed.

"I don't think you're going to have any trouble eating. If the thought of food makes you that hungry and not sick, you should have no problem eating it." The knock at the door sounded like a drum, but the food getting close to him made it easier to ignore it. "And yes, you're my child. But not just mine. Holly's as well. She fed you your last blood to convert you. I wasn't here and you needed it."

The tray was set on the table and Myles nearly snarled at the man who opened the shiny covers to reveal it. He picked up the burger and took a bite. The only issue he had was wondering if he could stuff all three of them in his mouth at once.

After he finished off the last one, he leaned back in his chair. Everything seemed to be right with the world all of a sudden. Myles looked over at Phil, who'd not said a thing since he'd picked up his first burger. He felt badly for all the horrible thoughts he'd had about killing him the past two days and decided he could almost forgive him. Maybe.

"You can't. Kill me, that is. As your maker, you cannot cause me harm. It's been done, as you know, but not with intent." Phil tossed him a book. "There's a sort of manual. It's not really a great deal of help, but it is a fun read. The author writes smut books and is actually a vampire herself. She puts a lot of fiction in there for her readers."

Myles looked at the cover and knew that he'd seen this particular author's picture on a lot of bookstore fronts. He tossed it on the bed and looked at Phil.

"You can read my mind. Is that because you made me or what?" Myles found he wasn't as freaked out as he probably should have been. "And will that fade too?"

"Yes, both Holly and I will be able to read your mind. Find you, as well, and feel your emotions. Will we intrude? Probably for the first few years until you get your life together. After that...." Phil shrugged. "That'll be up to you. And no, it doesn't fade, but the trust between us makes it less of an intrusion."

They talked for another hour. Myles felt better by the time Phil stood to go. He shook his hand when it was offered. But he was sure that Phil wouldn't be so easy to get along with if he fucked up.

"I'm glad you're going to be around. Life will be interesting, as well as hard work." He turned to go then looked back. "Oh, I've spoken with Gordon Force, Holly's brother. He is starting up an investigating firm and is willing to take you on if you'd like."

Myles was nodding even before Phil finished. "I'll take it. I need to…I'm not used to being idle."

"You won't be. If you need me, you only have to think of me answering you and I'll be there. And Holly?" Myles waited. He knew what was coming next. "You'd better have a good reason for calling my mate."

Myles threw back his head and laughed. Maybe being a vampire wouldn't be so bad after all. He picked up the book after Phil left and started reading.

Melody looked at Marcus. She had never been so unsure of anything in all her considerable life. As queen, it wasn't something she wanted to happen again either.

"Are you sure about this? She's just a child, not even a teenager yet. Why do you think this…this little girl has what hundreds, no, thousands don't?"

Marcus, her Man at Arms of her Royal Guard, grinned.

ABOUT THE AUTHOR

Hello! My name is Kathi Barton and I'm an author. I have been married to my very best friend Sonny for at times seems several lifetimes – in a good way, honey. And together we have three wonderful children and then the ones we brought into the world - Paul and Dale Barton, Jason and Wendy Barton and Danielle and Ben Conklin. They have given us seven of the greatest treasures on Earth. They don't live at home seven days a week! No, seriously, seven grandchildren – Gavin, Spring, Ben, Trinity, Sarah, Kelly and Kian.

Follow Kathi on her blog:
http://kathisbartonauthor.blogspot.com/

)

www.ingramcontent.com/pod-product-compliance
Lightning Source LLC
Chambersburg PA
CBHW020616180626
46810CB00007B/2803